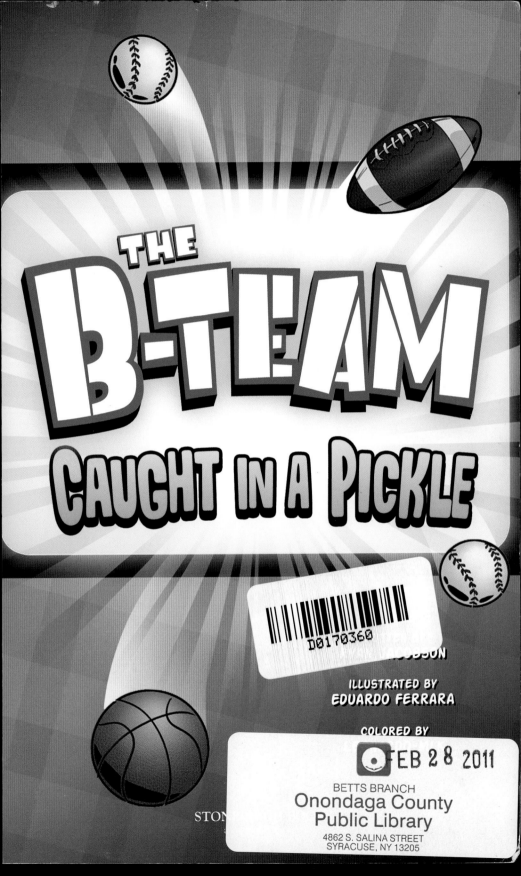

THE B-TEAM

CAUGHT IN A PICKLE

ILLUSTRATED BY
EDUARDO FERRARA

COLORED BY

During tryouts, four young athletes didn't make the cut.

But even when their teams gave up on them . . .

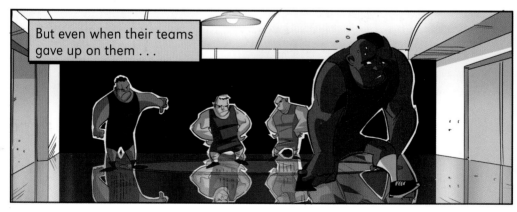

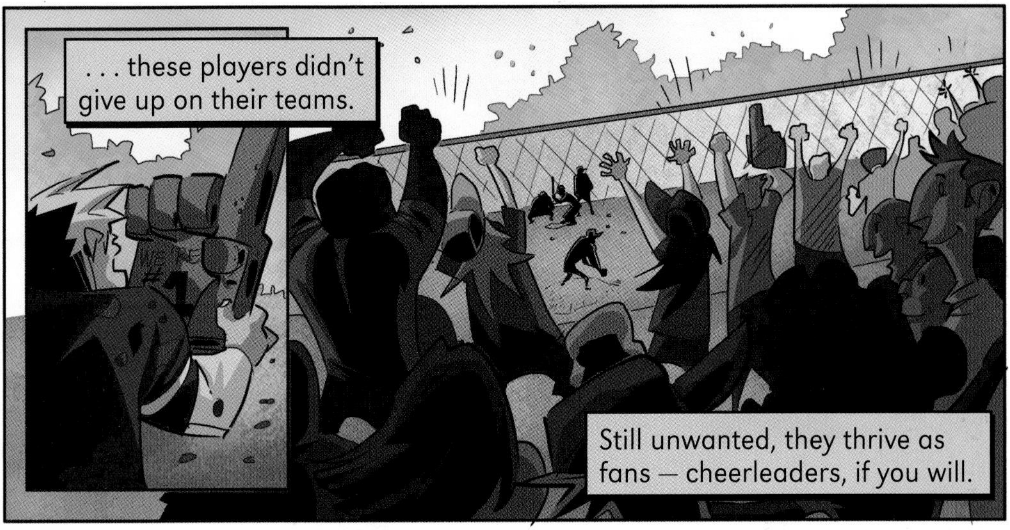
. . . these players didn't give up on their teams.
WE'RE #1
Still unwanted, they thrive as fans — cheerleaders, if you will.

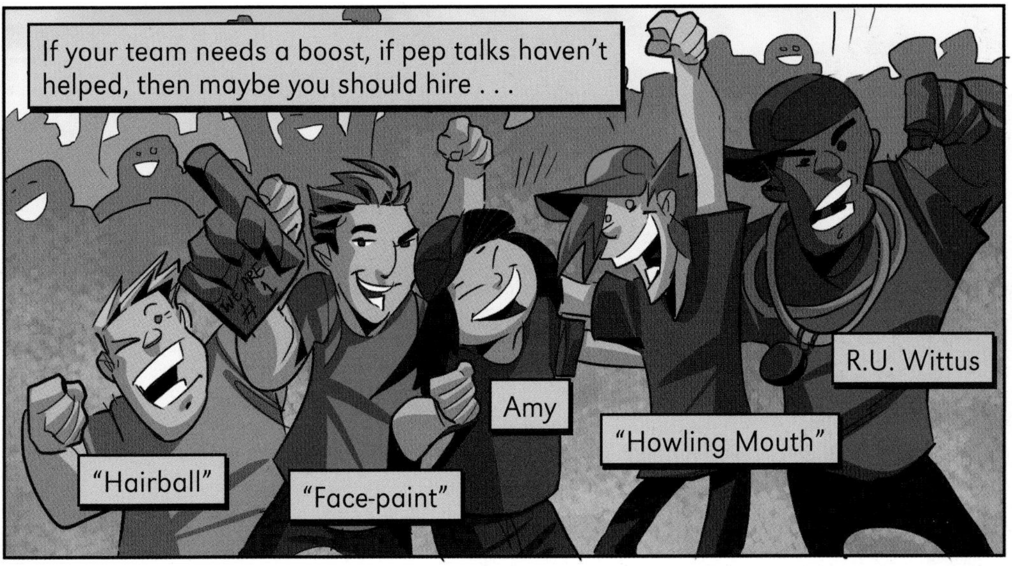
If your team needs a boost, if pep talks haven't helped, then maybe you should hire . . .
R.U. Wittus
Amy
"Howling Mouth"
"Hairball"
"Face-paint"

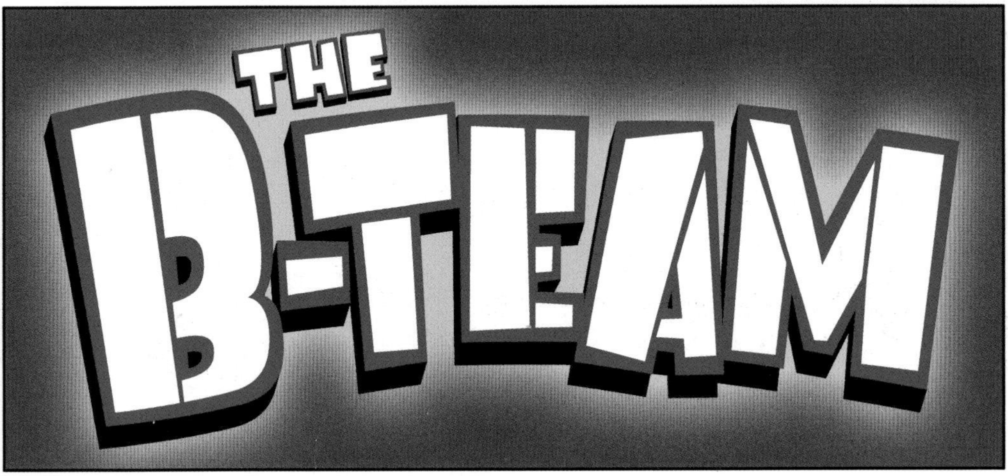
THE
B-TEAM

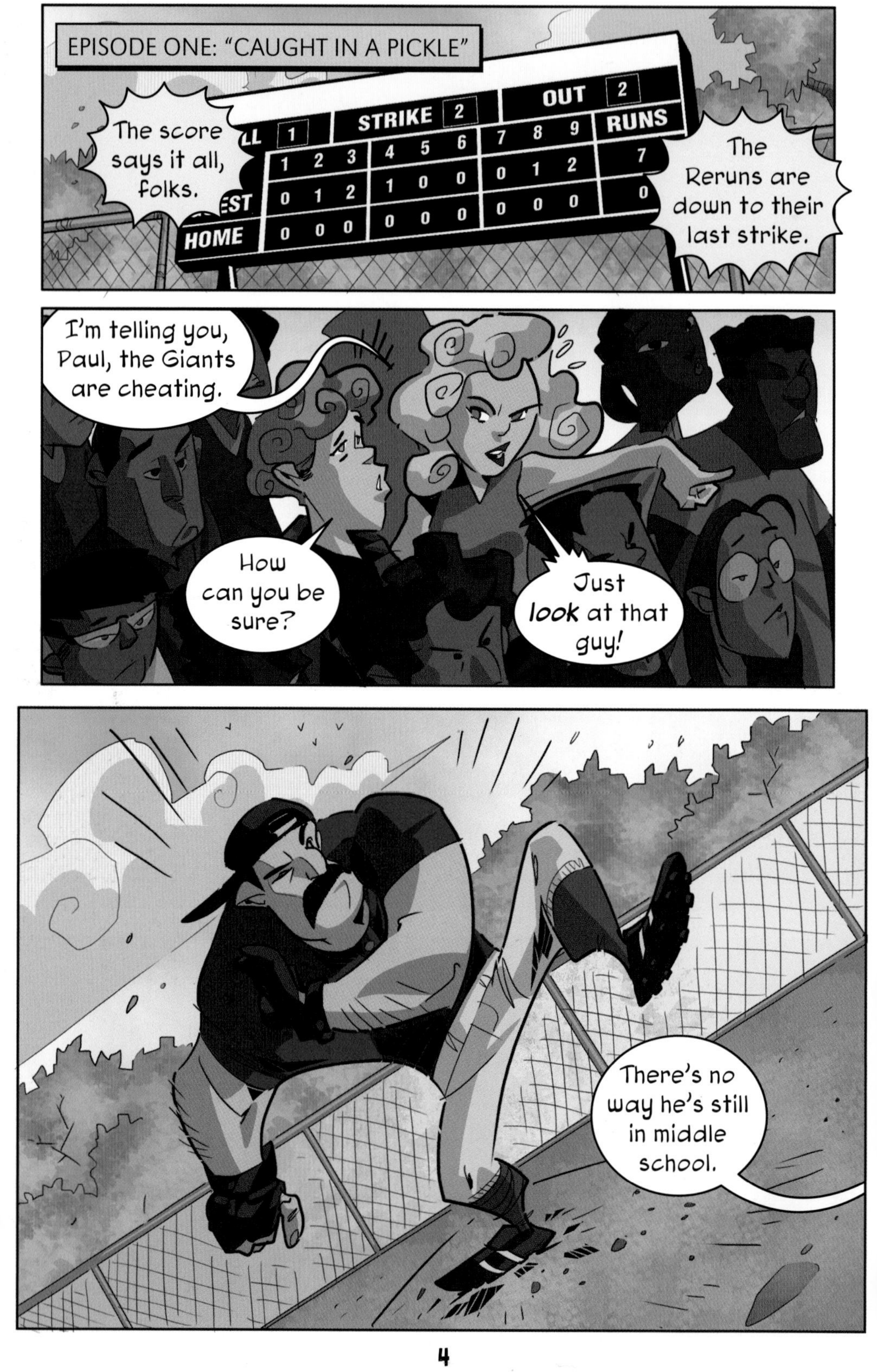
EPISODE ONE: "CAUGHT IN A PICKLE"
The score says it all, folks.
STRIKE 2
OUT 2
RUNS
HOME
The Reruns are down to their last strike.
I'm telling you, Paul, the Giants are cheating.
How can you be sure?
Just look at that guy!
There's no way he's still in middle school.

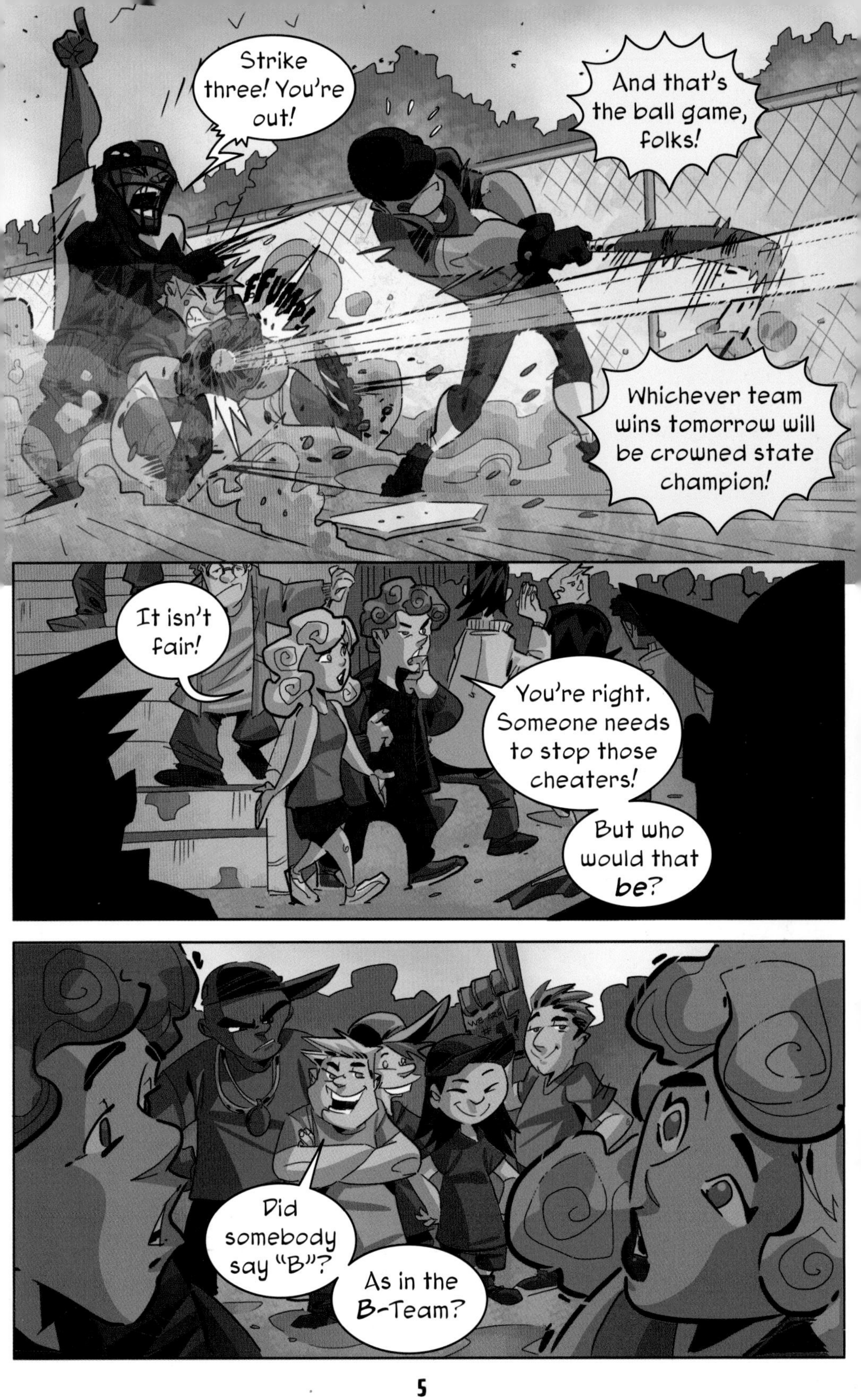
Strike three! You're out!
And that's the ball game, folks!
FFUMP!
Whichever team wins tomorrow will be crowned state champion!
It isn't fair!
You're right. Someone needs to stop those cheaters!
But who would that *be*?
Did somebody say "B"?
As in the *B*-Team?

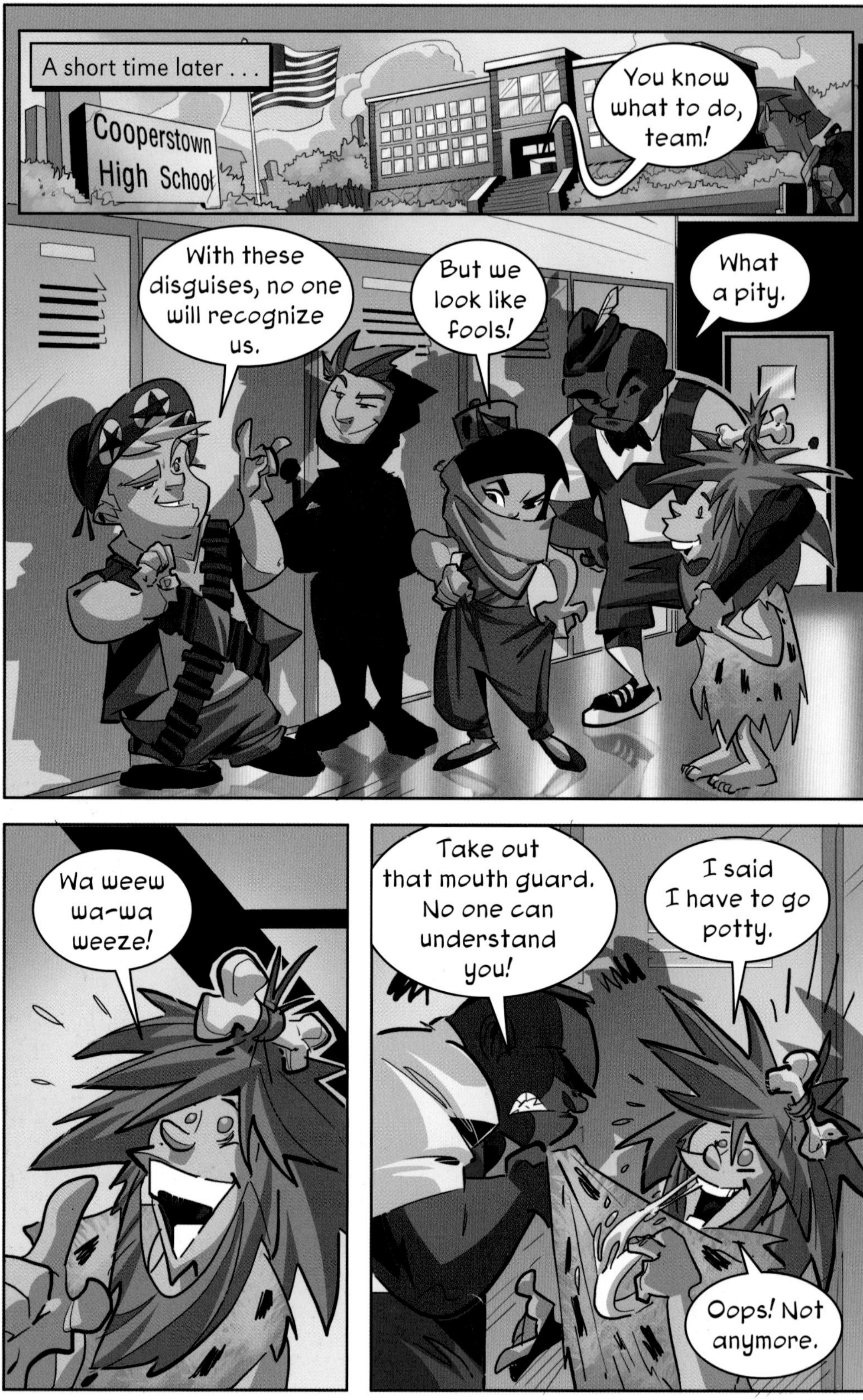
A short time later . . .
Cooperstown High School
You know what to do, team!
With these disguises, no one will recognize us.
But we look like fools!
What a pity.
Wa weew wa-wa weeze!
Take out that mouth guard. No one can understand you!
I said I have to go potty.
Oops! Not anymore.

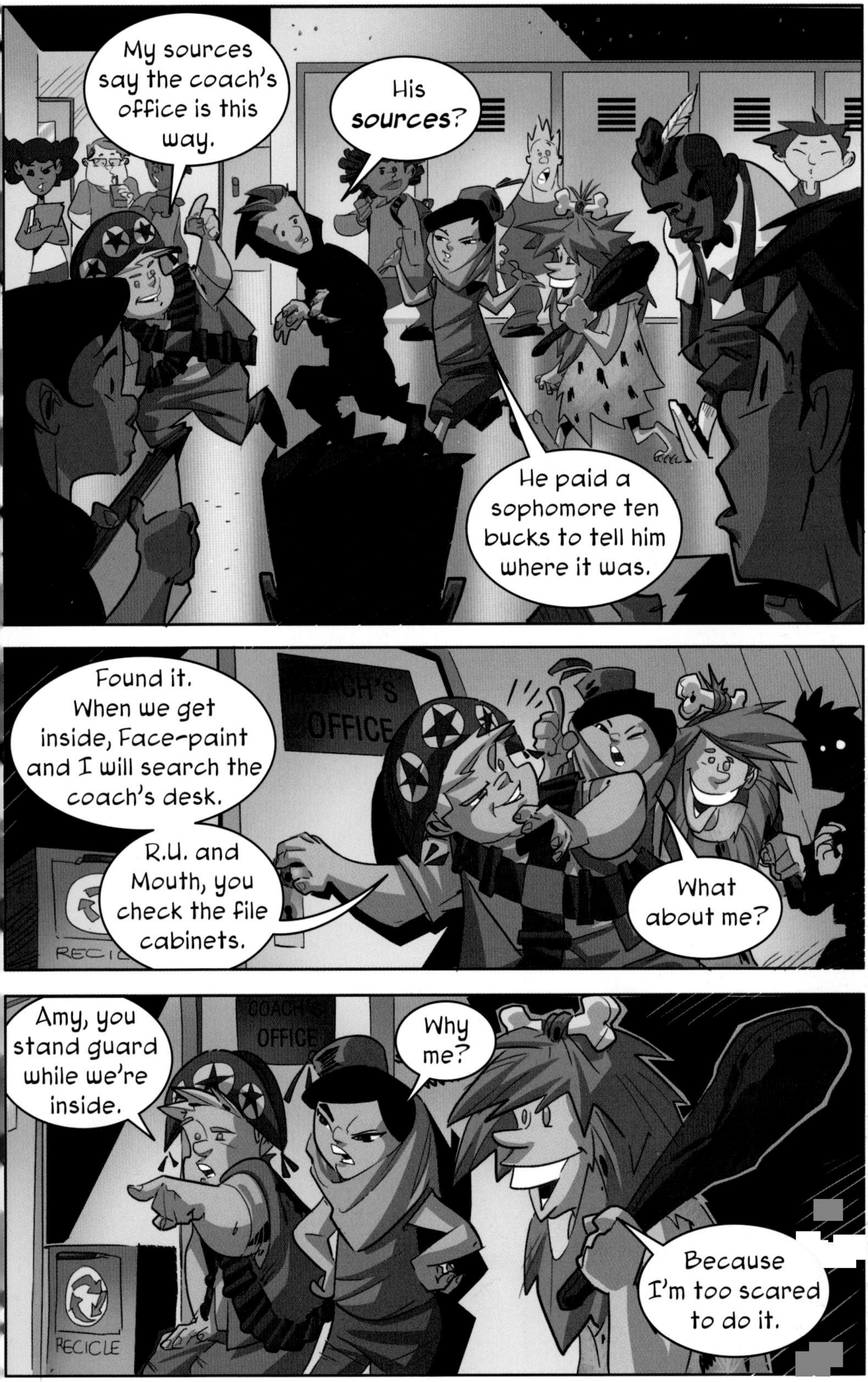
My sources say the coach's office is this way.
His **sources**?
He paid a sophomore ten bucks to tell him where it was.
OFFICE
Found it. When we get inside, Face-paint and I will search the coach's desk.
R.U. and Mouth, you check the file cabinets.
What about me?
COACH'S OFFICE
Amy, you stand guard while we're inside.
Why me?
Because I'm too scared to do it.
RECICLE

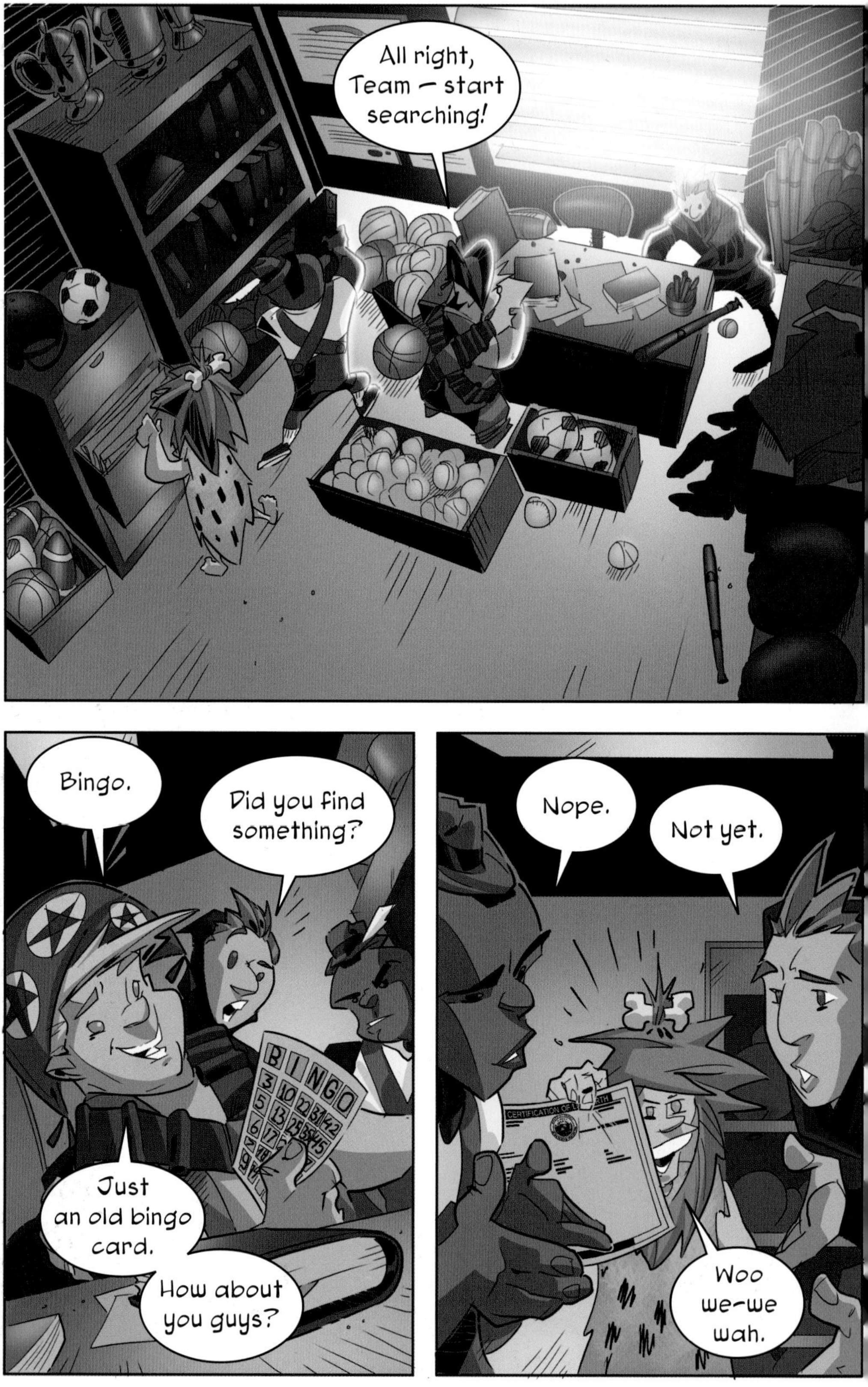

All right, Team — start searching!
Bingo.
Did you find something?
BINGO
Just an old bingo card.
How about you guys?
Nope.
Not yet.
Woo we-we wah.

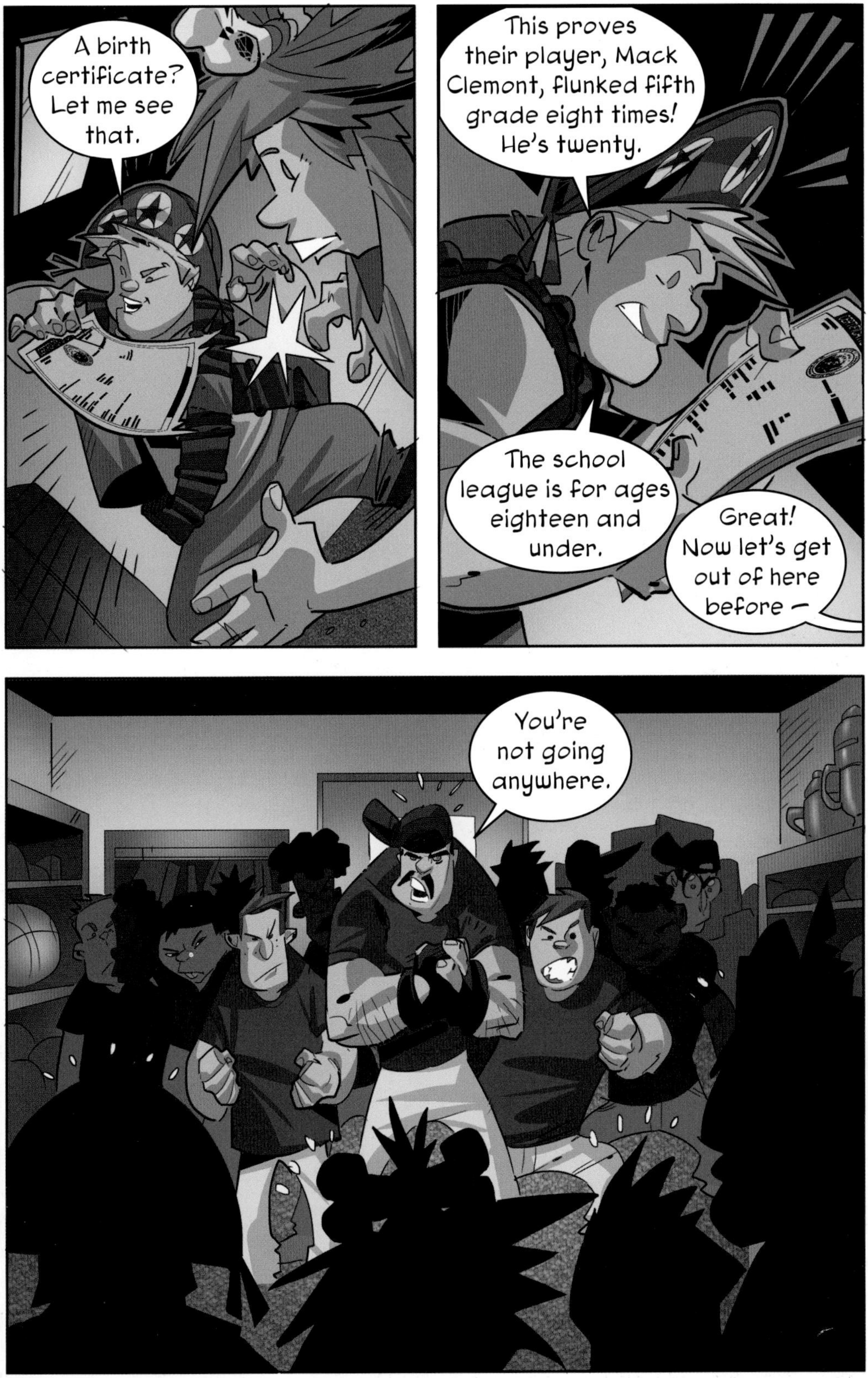
A birth certificate? Let me see that.
This proves their player, Mack Clemont, flunked fifth grade eight times! He's twenty.
The school league is for ages eighteen and under.
Great! Now let's get out of here before —
You're not going anywhere.

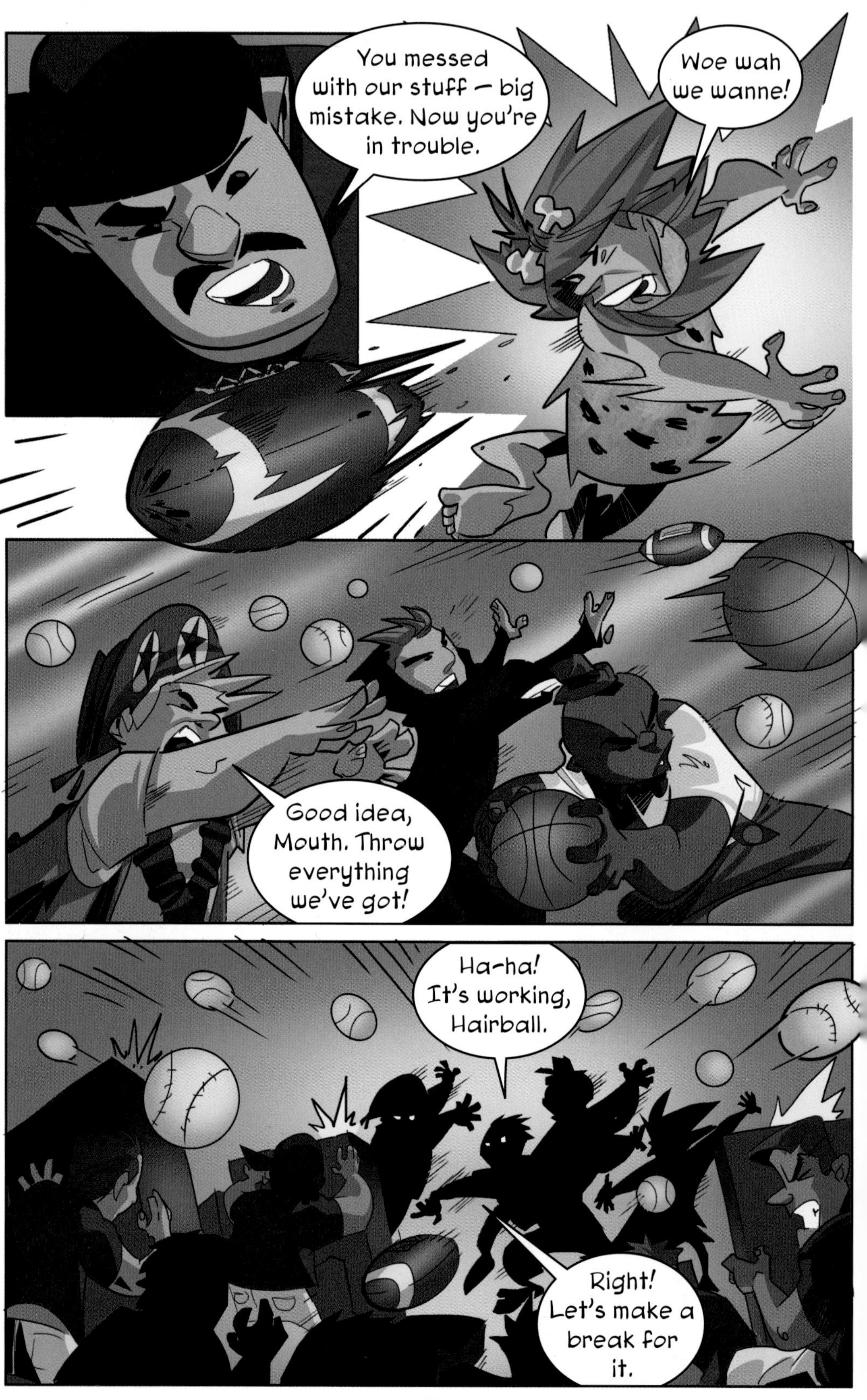

You messed with our stuff — big mistake. Now you're in trouble.
Woe wah we wanne!
Good idea, Mouth. Throw everything we've got!
Ha-ha! It's working, Hairball.
Right! Let's make a break for it.

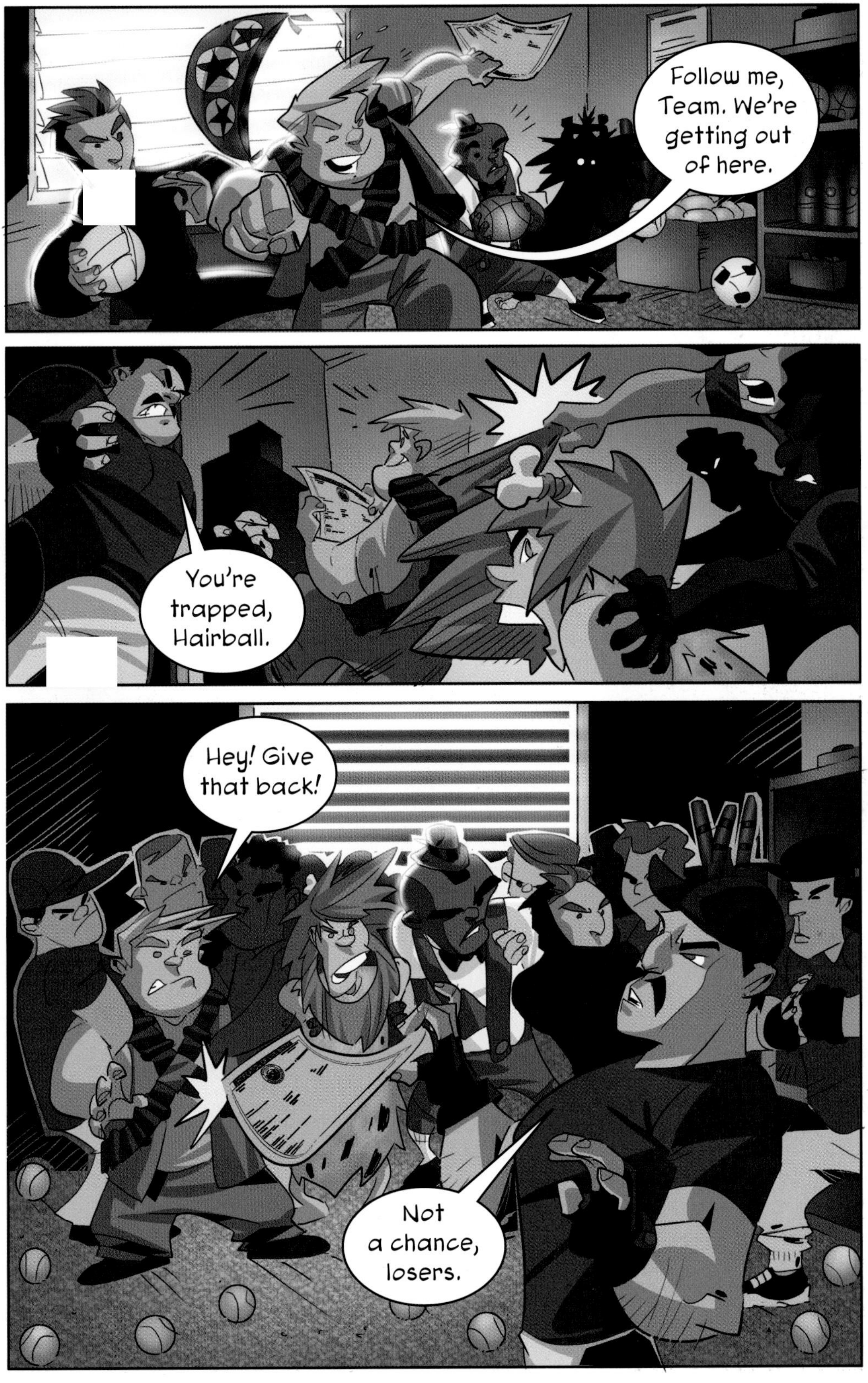
Follow me, Team. We're getting out of here.
You're trapped, Hairball.
Hey! Give that back!
Not a chance, losers.

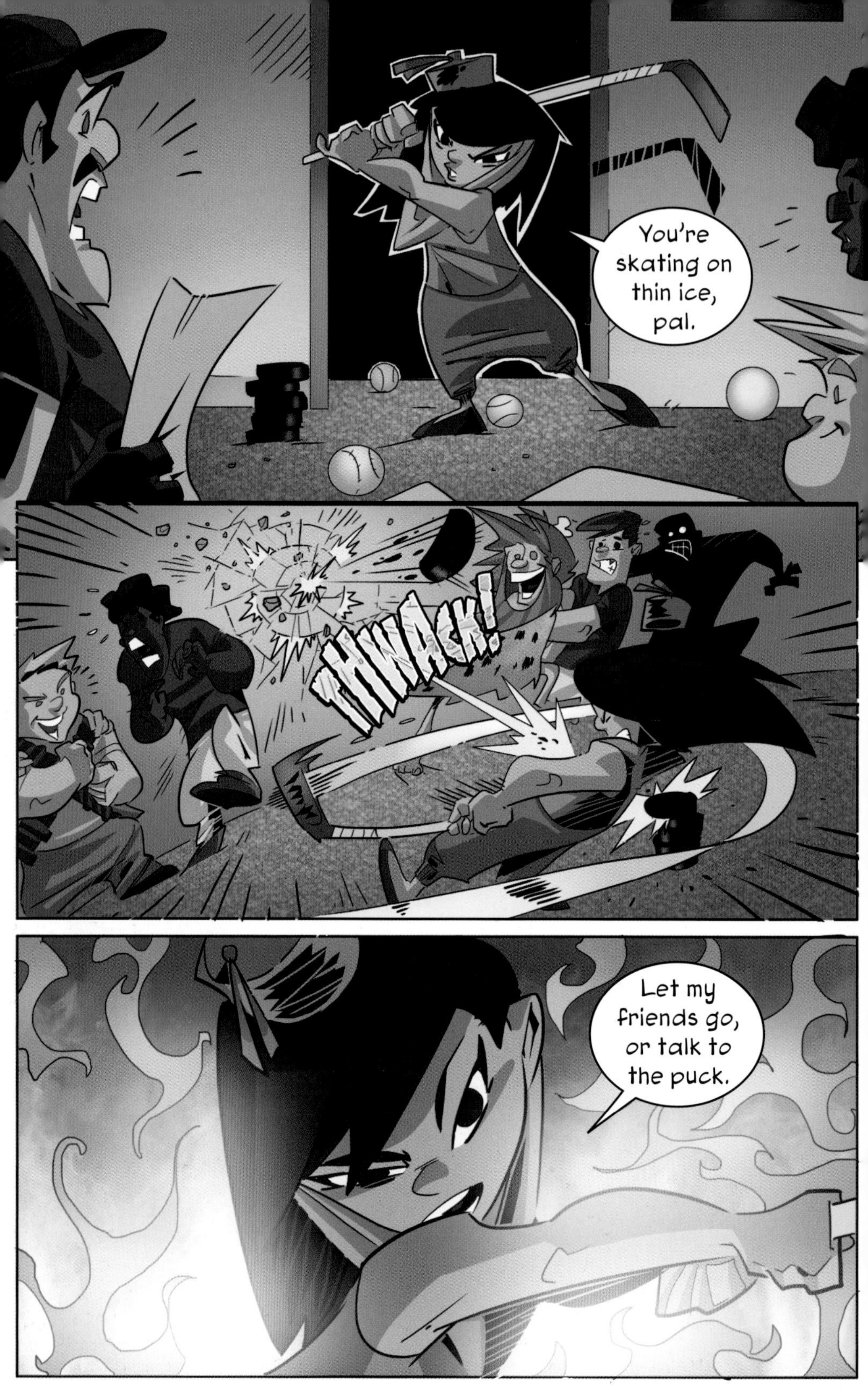

You're skating on thin ice, pal.
THWACK!
Let my friends go, or talk to the puck.

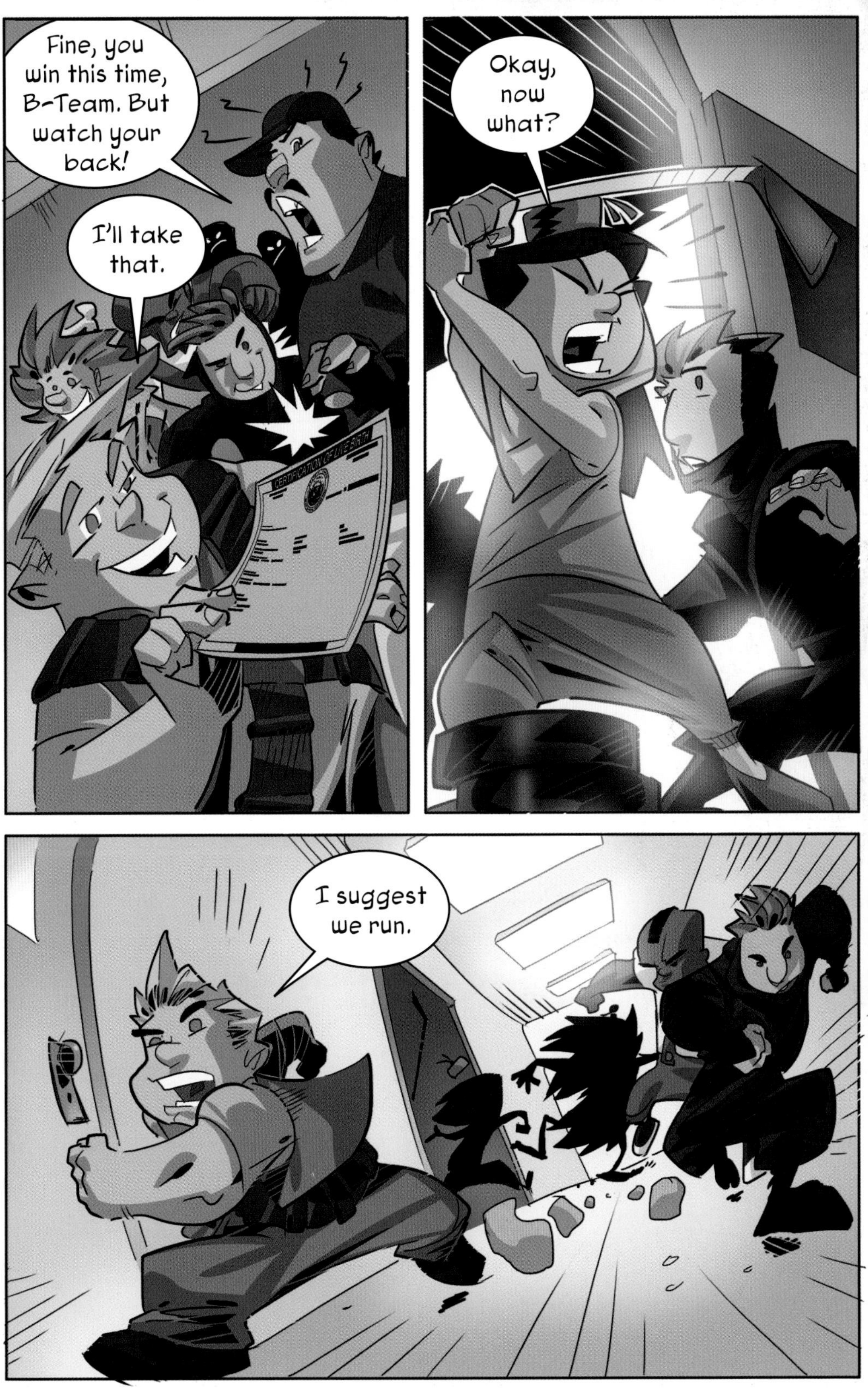
Fine, you win this time, B-Team. But watch your back!
I'll take that.
CERTIFICATION OF LIVE BIRTH
Okay, now what?
I suggest we run.

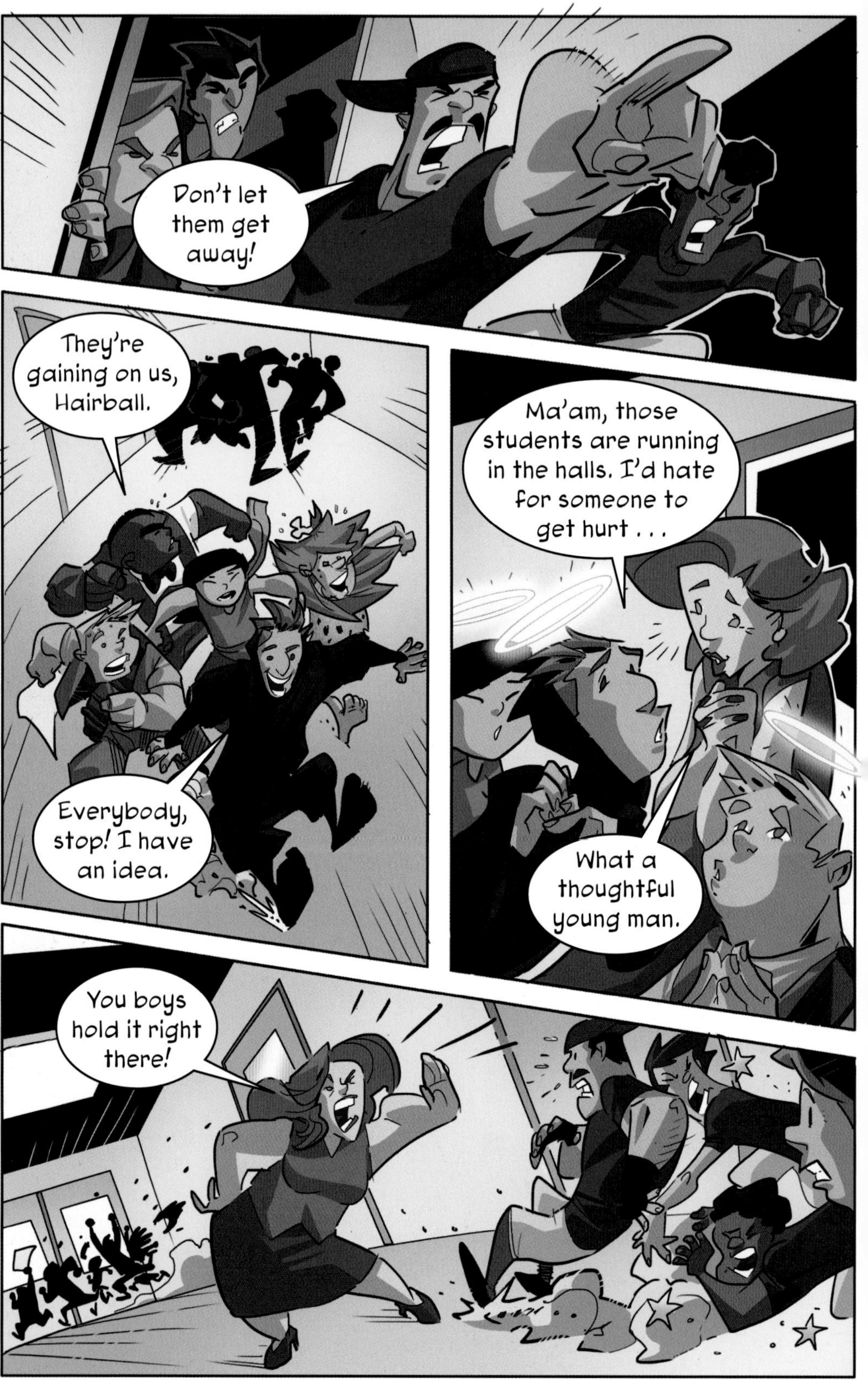
Don't let them get away!
They're gaining on us, Hairball.
Everybody, stop! I have an idea.
Ma'am, those students are running in the halls. I'd hate for someone to get hurt . . .
What a thoughtful young man.
You boys hold it right there!

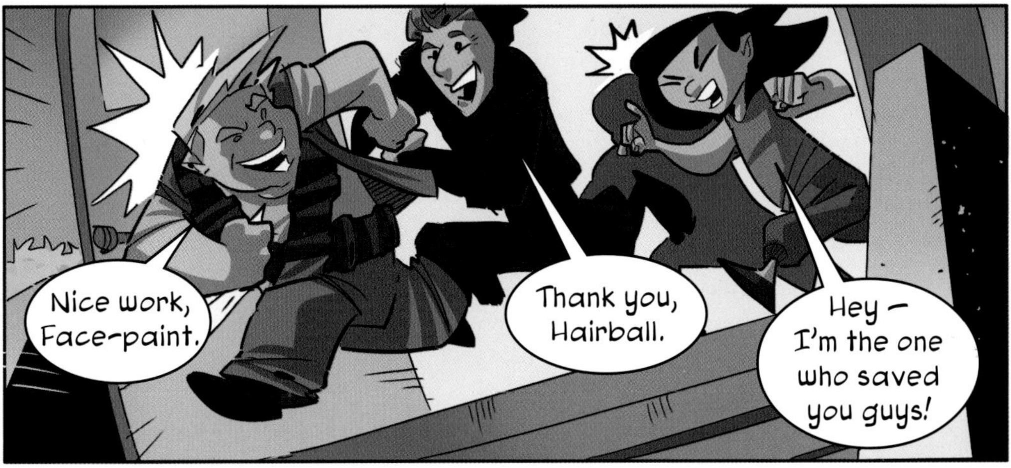
Nice work, Face-paint.
Thank you, Hairball.
Hey — I'm the one who saved you guys!

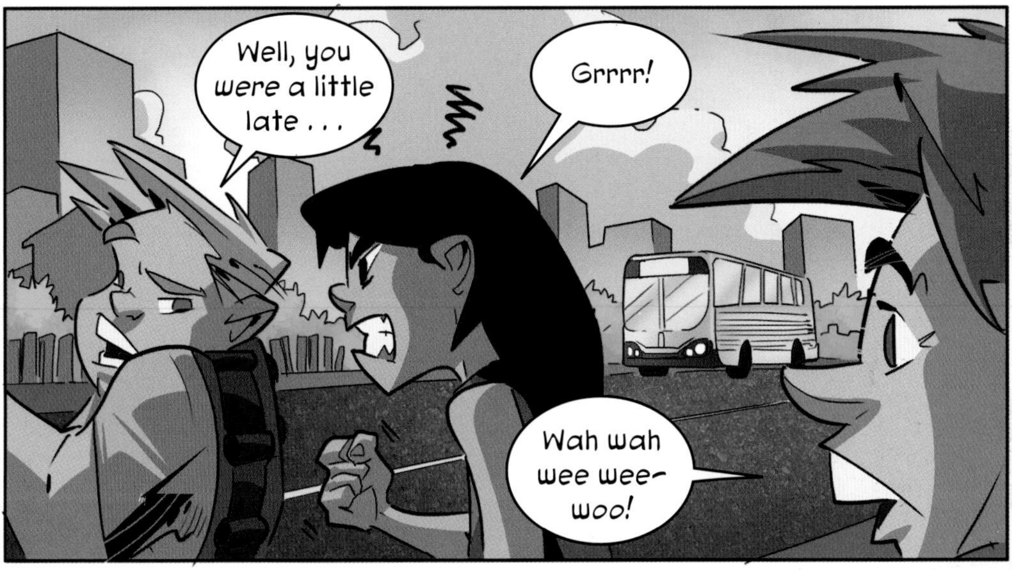
Well, you were a little late . . .
Grrrr!
Wah wah wee wee-woo!

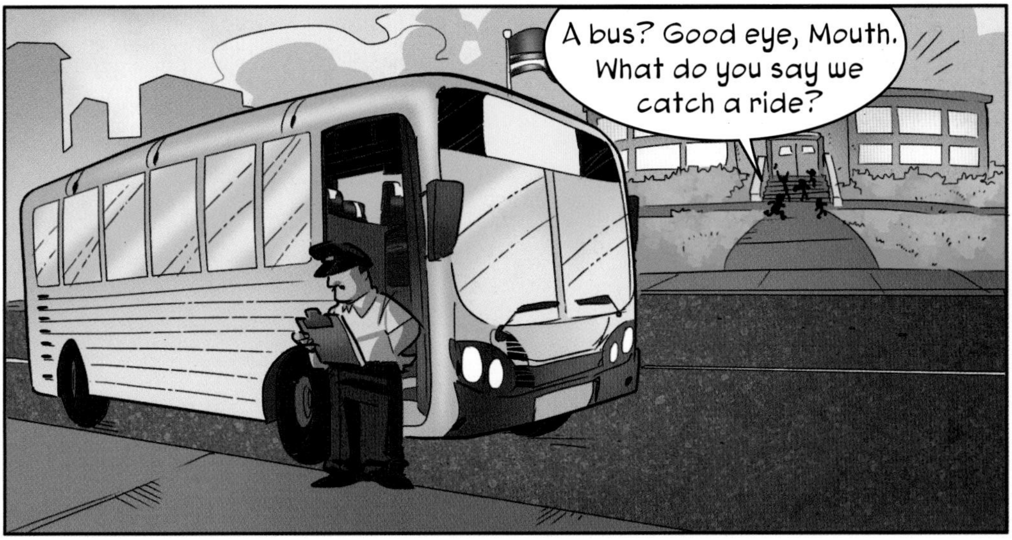
A bus? Good eye, Mouth. What do you say we catch a ride?

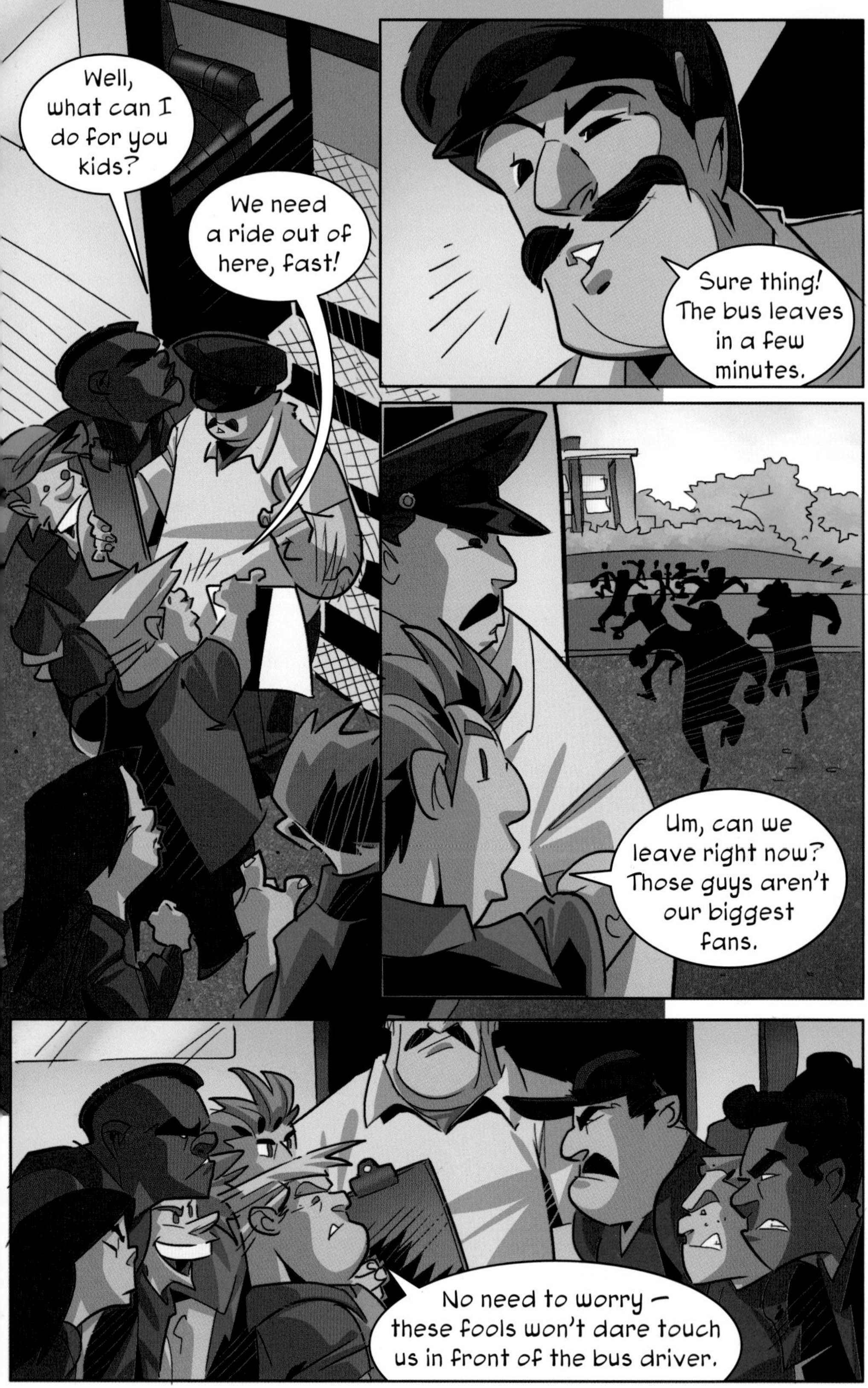
Well, what can I do for you kids?
We need a ride out of here, fast!
Sure thing! The bus leaves in a few minutes.
Um, can we leave right now? Those guys aren't our biggest fans.
No need to worry — these fools won't dare touch us in front of the bus driver.

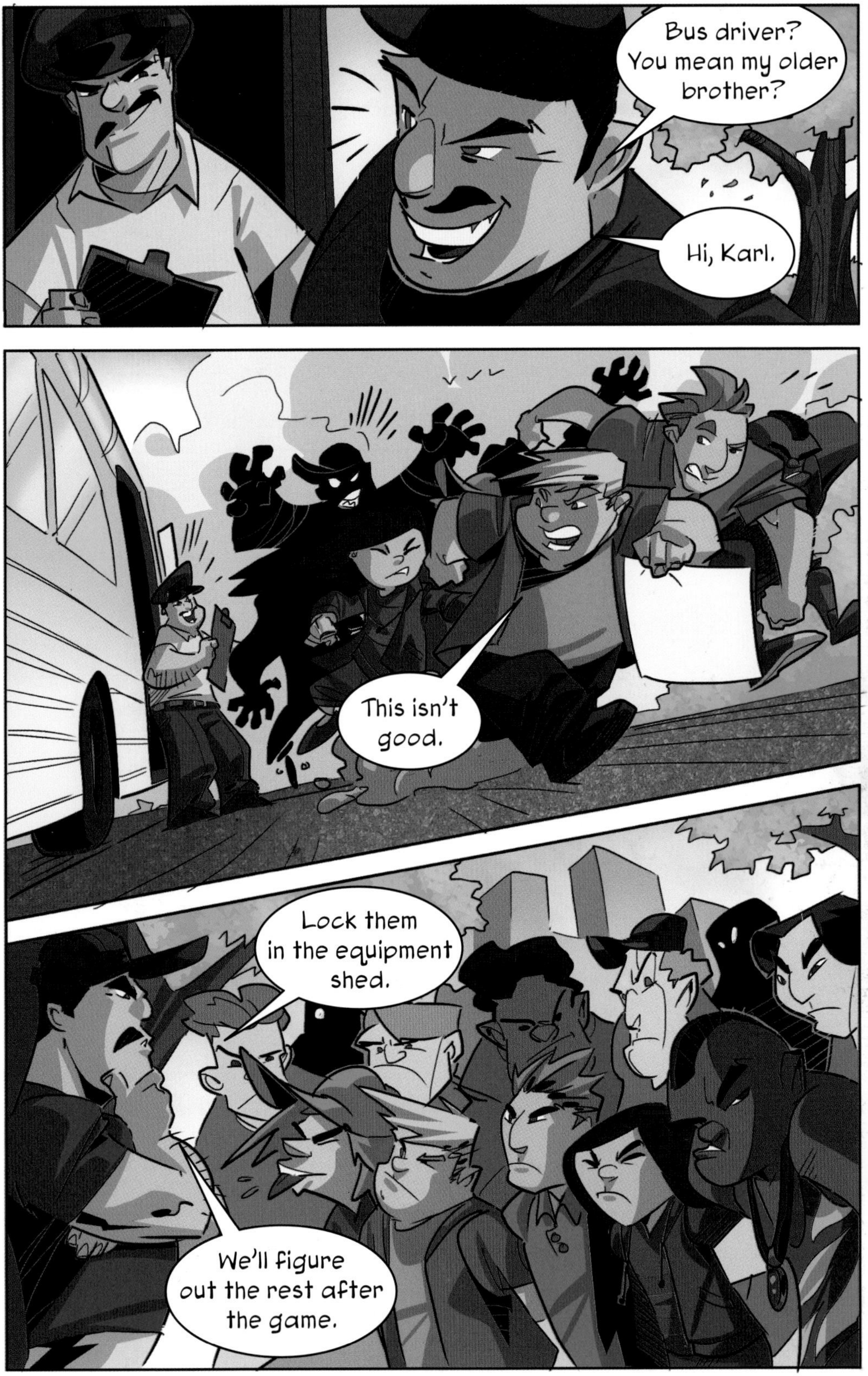
Bus driver? You mean my older brother?
Hi, Karl.
This isn't good.
Lock them in the equipment shed.
We'll figure out the rest after the game.

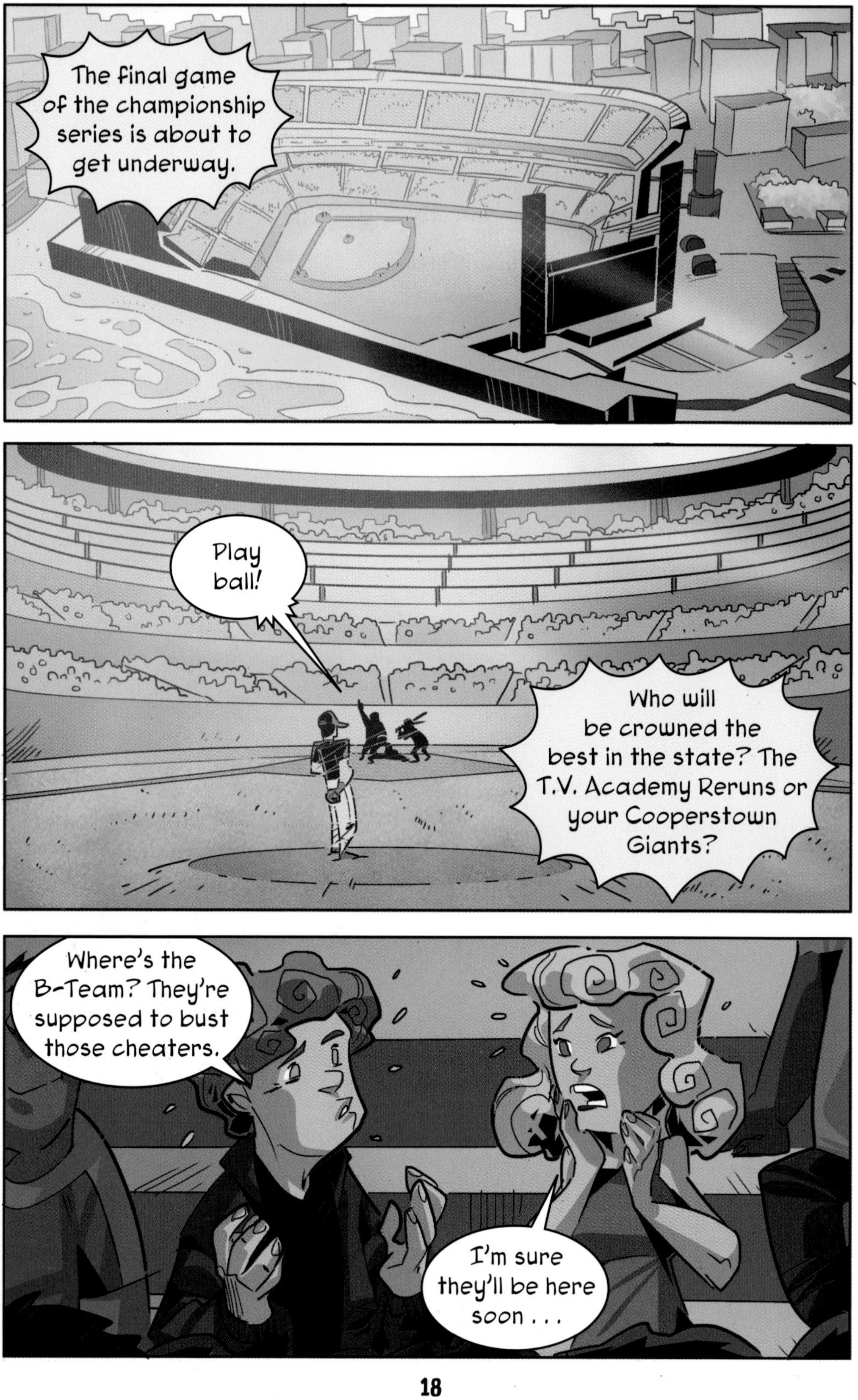
The final game of the championship series is about to get underway.
Play ball!
Who will be crowned the best in the state? The T.V. Academy Reruns or your Cooperstown Giants?
Where's the B-Team? They're supposed to bust those cheaters.
I'm sure they'll be here soon . . .

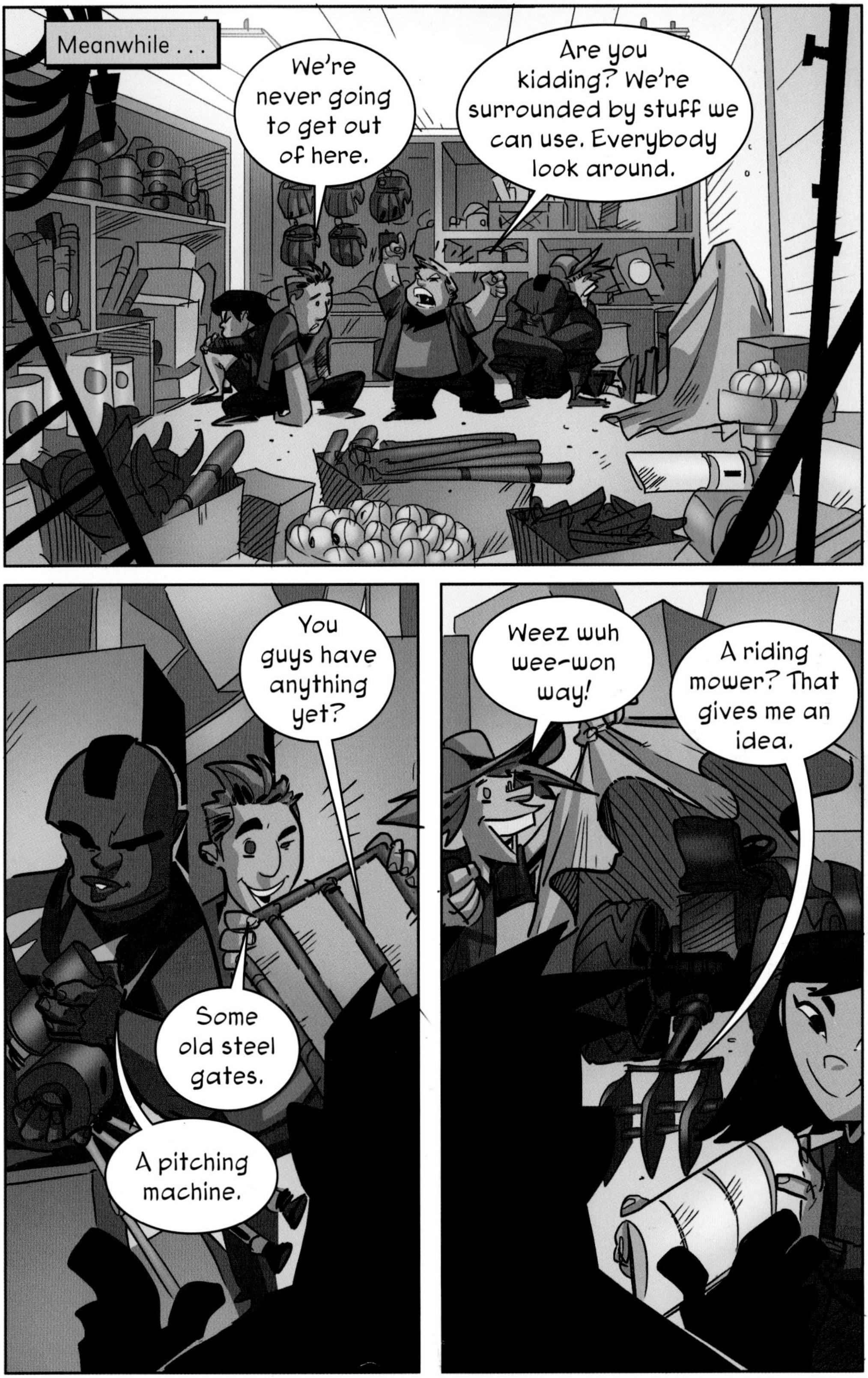
Meanwhile . . .
We're never going to get out of here.
Are you kidding? We're surrounded by stuff we can use. Everybody look around.
You guys have anything yet?
Some old steel gates.
A pitching machine.
Weez wuh wee-won way!
A riding mower? That gives me an idea.

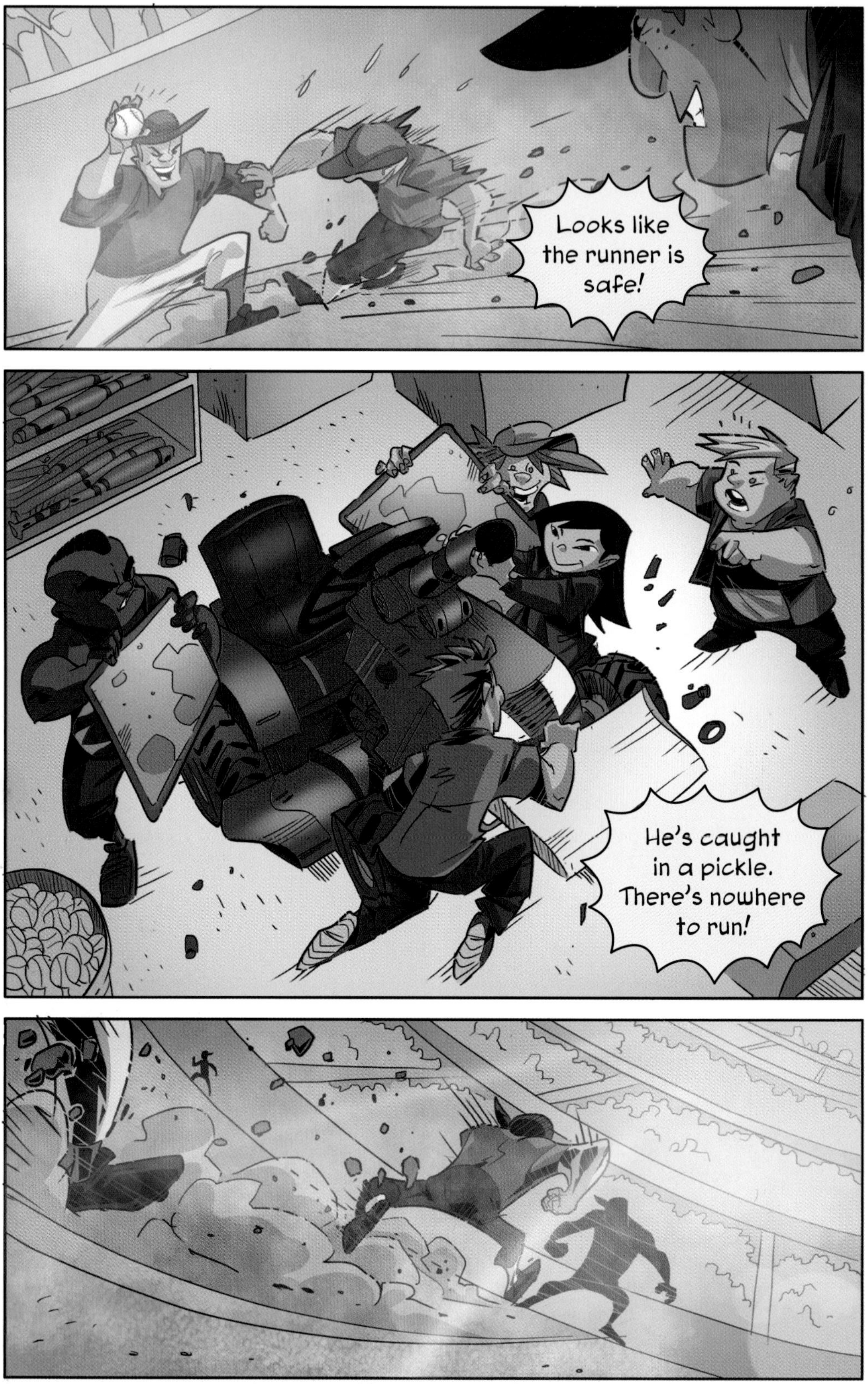
Looks like the runner is safe!
He's caught in a pickle. There's nowhere to run!

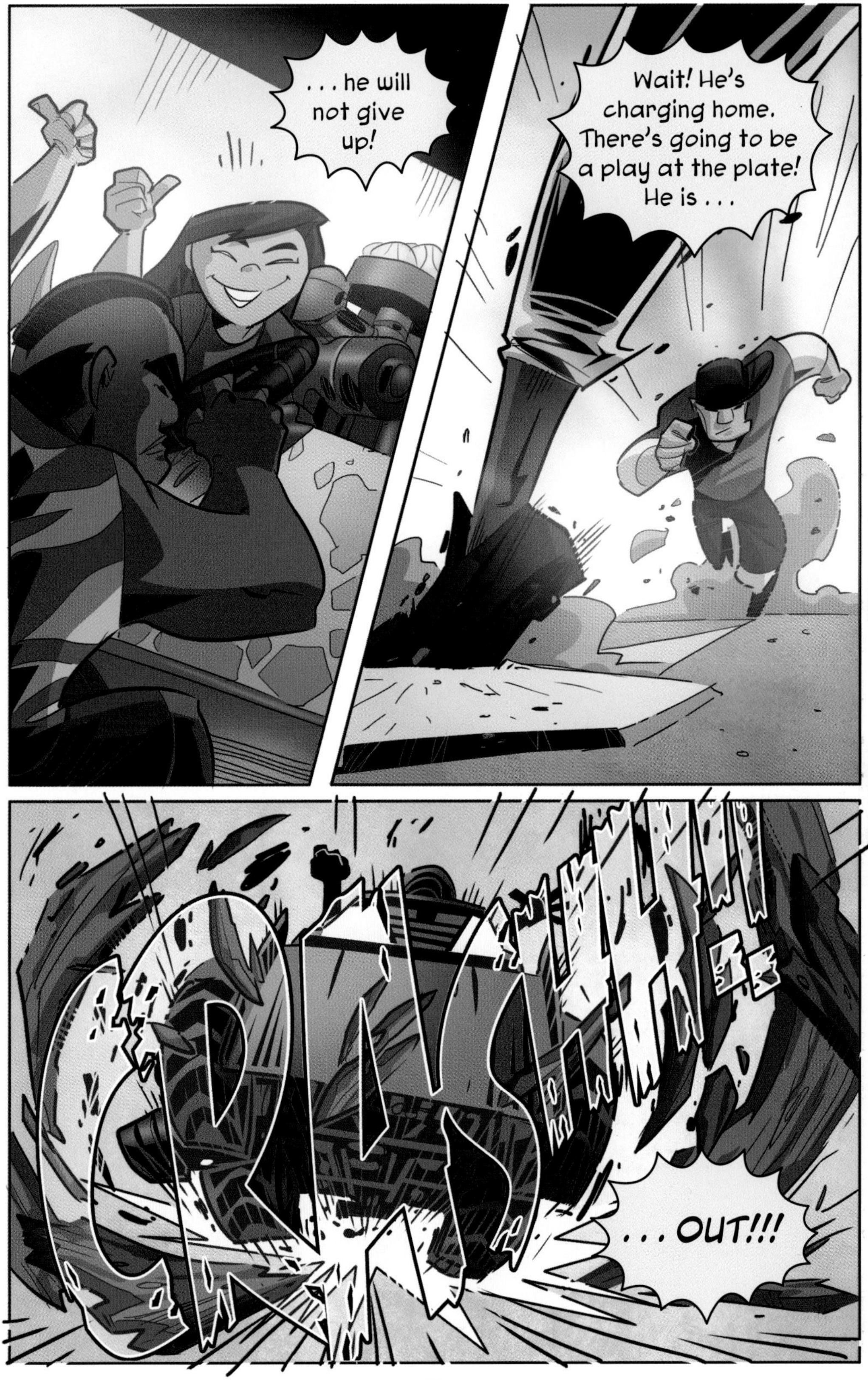
. . . he will not give up!
Wait! He's charging home. There's going to be a play at the plate! He is . . .
CRASH!
. . . OUT!!!

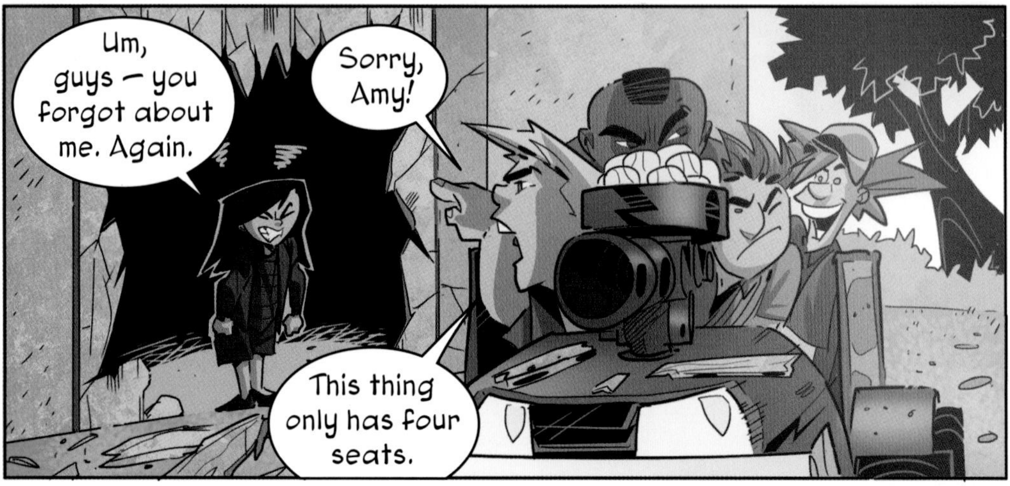
Um, guys — you forgot about me. Again.
Sorry, Amy!
This thing only has four seats.

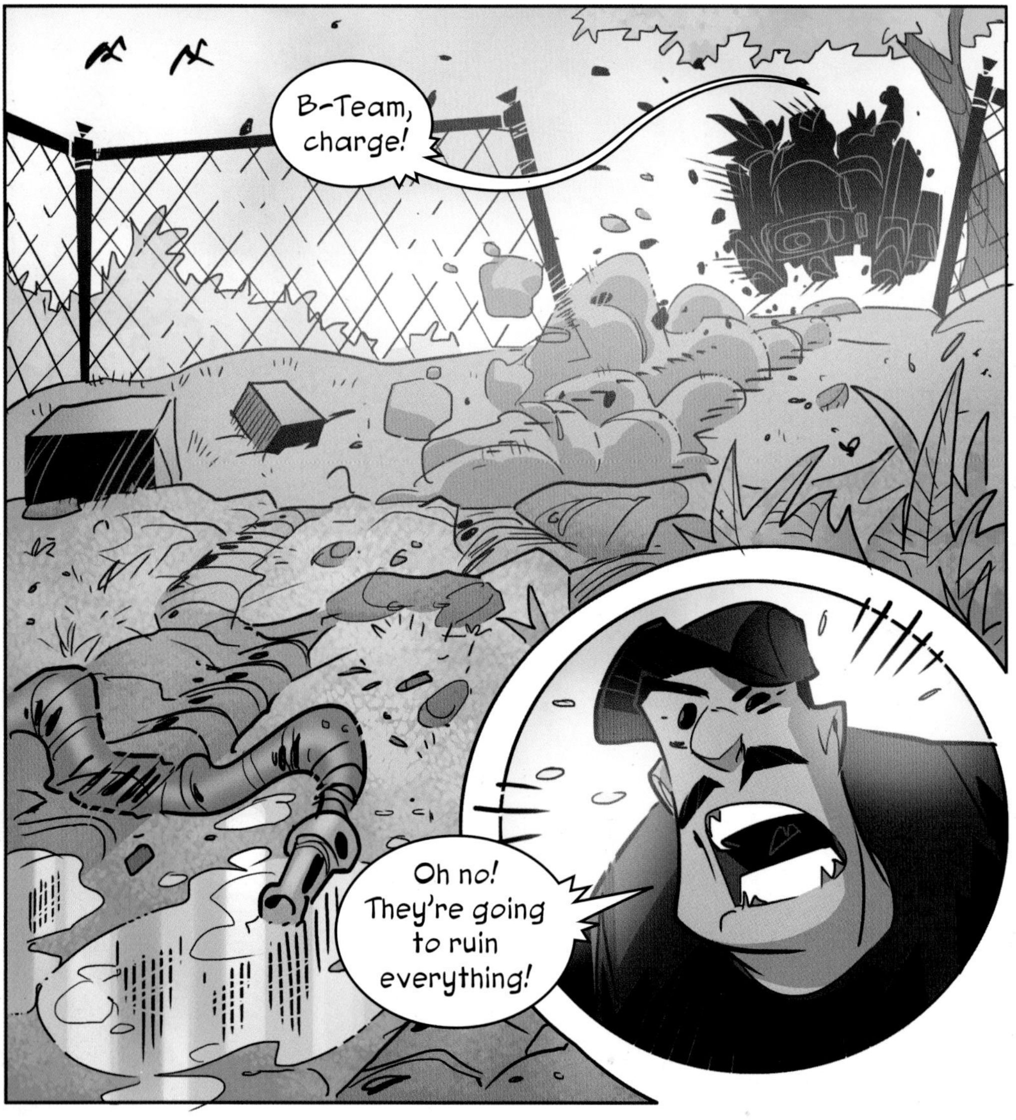
B-Team, charge!
Oh no! They're going to ruin everything!

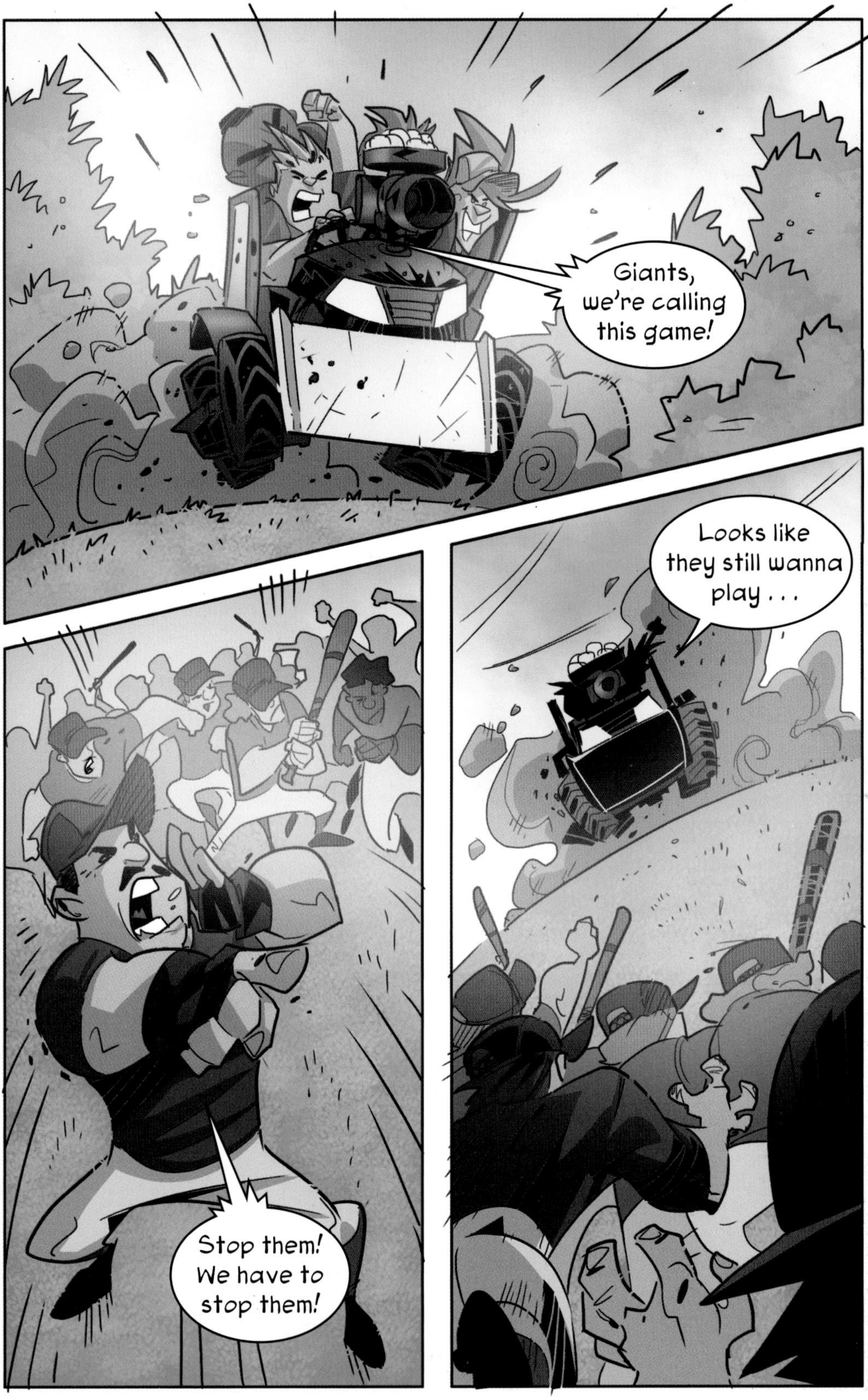
Giants, we're calling this game!
Stop them! We have to stop them!
Looks like they still wanna play . . .

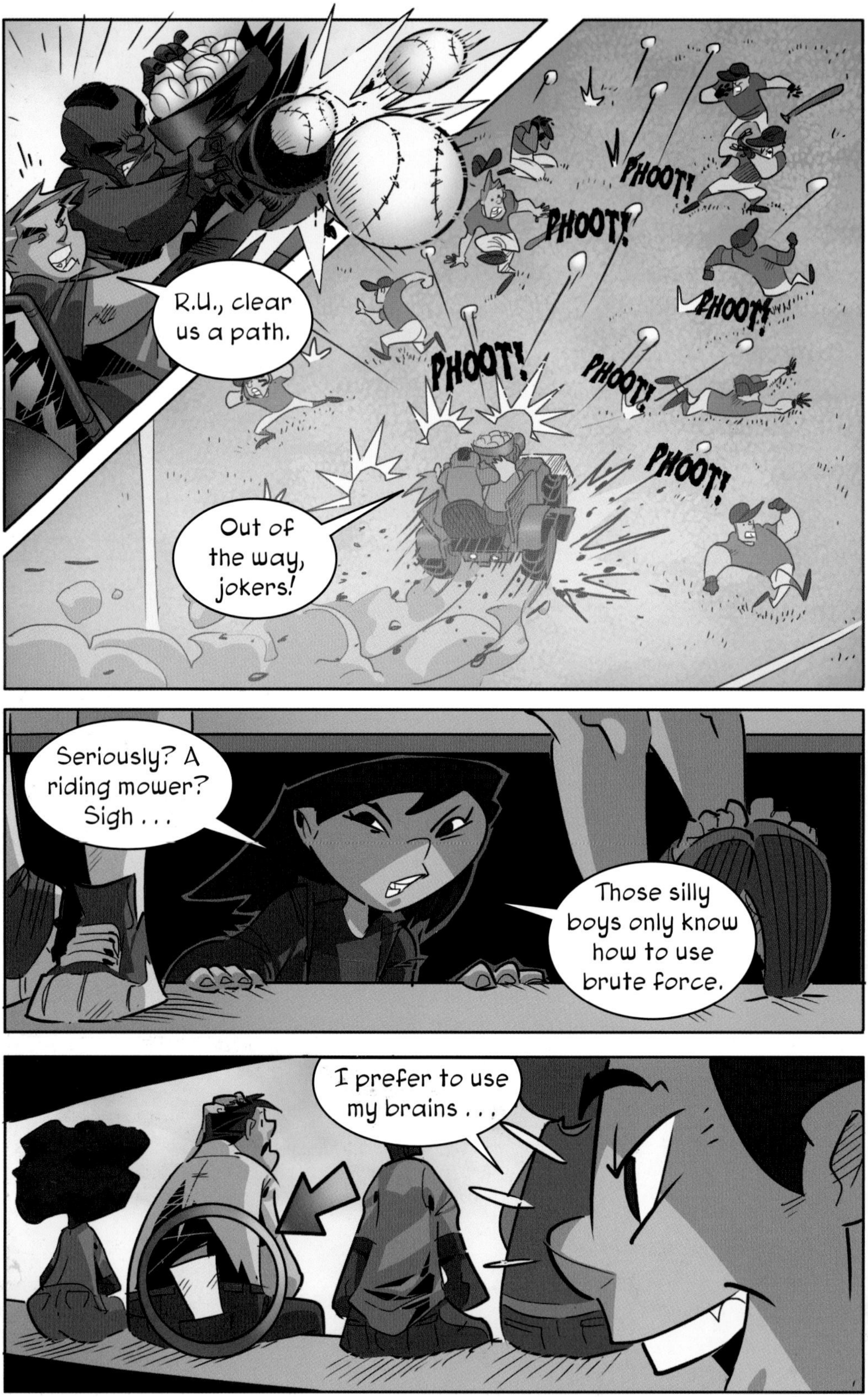
R.U., clear us a path.
PHOOT!
PHOOT!
PHOOT!
PHOOT!
PHOOT!
PHOOT!
Out of the way, jokers!
Seriously? A riding mower? Sigh . . .
Those silly boys only know how to use brute force.
I prefer to use my brains . . .

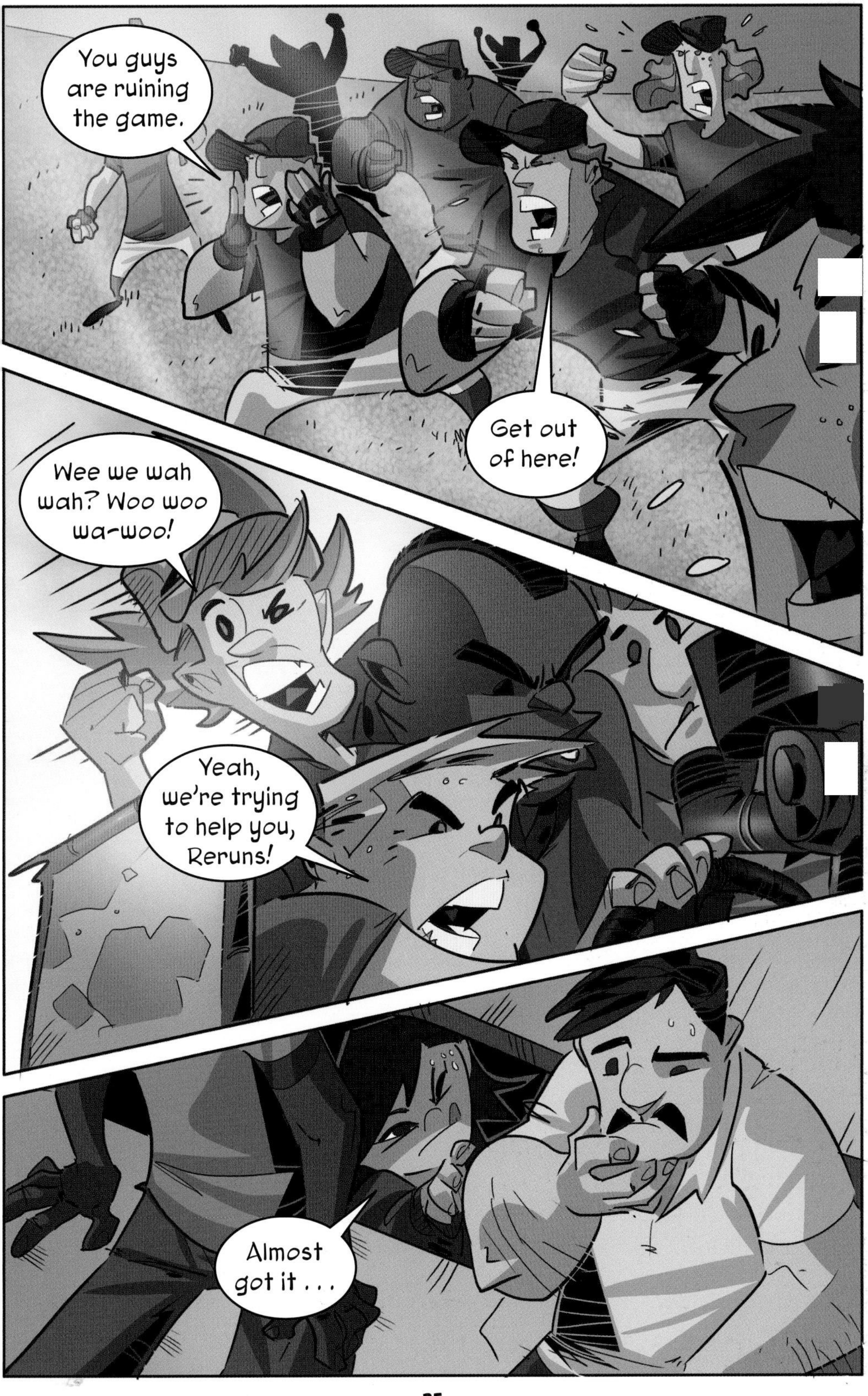
You guys are ruining the game.
Get out of here!
Wee we wah wah? Woo woo wa-woo!
Yeah, we're trying to help you, Reruns!
Almost got it . . .

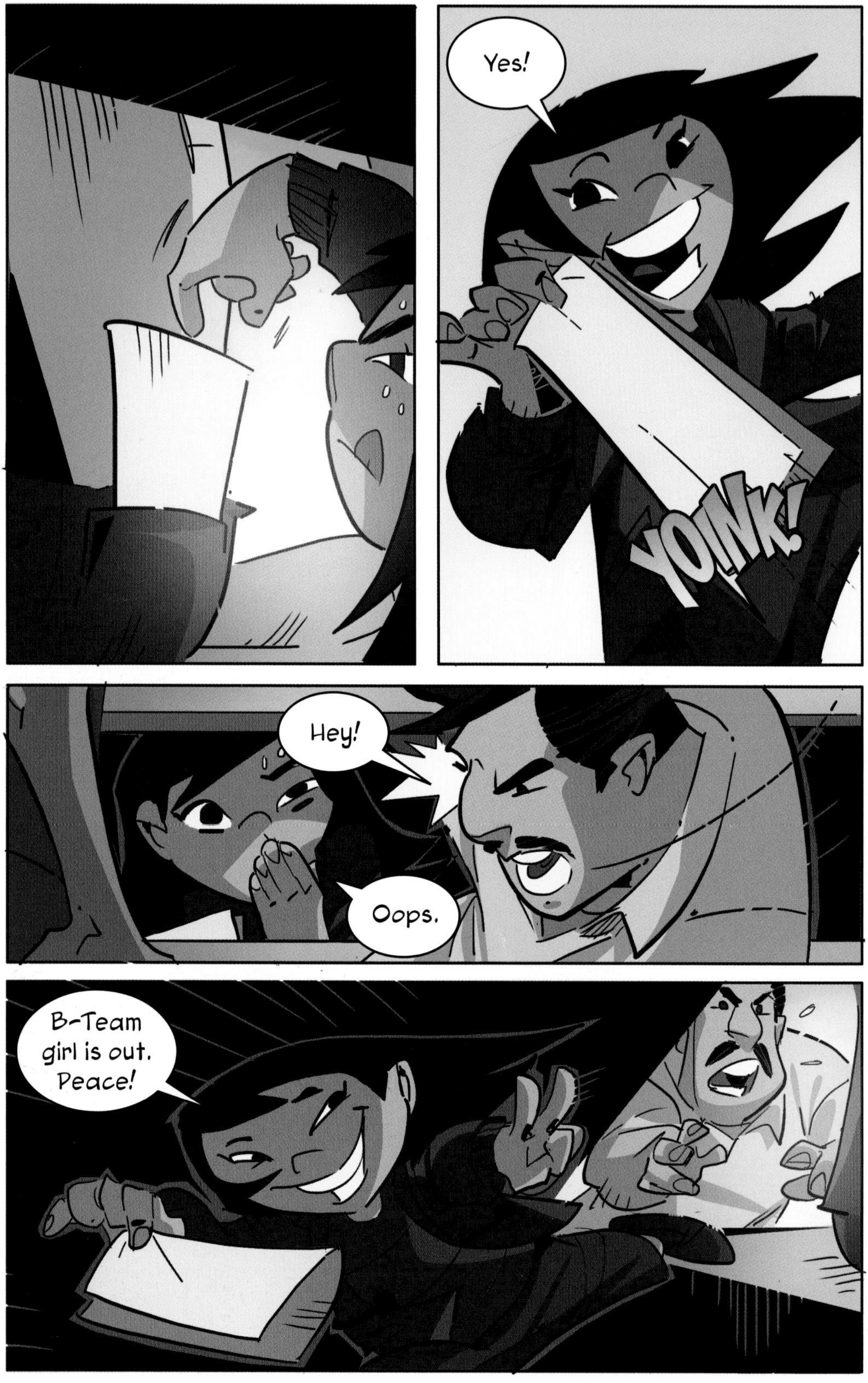

Yes!
YOINK!
Hey!
Oops.
B-Team
girl is out.
Peace!

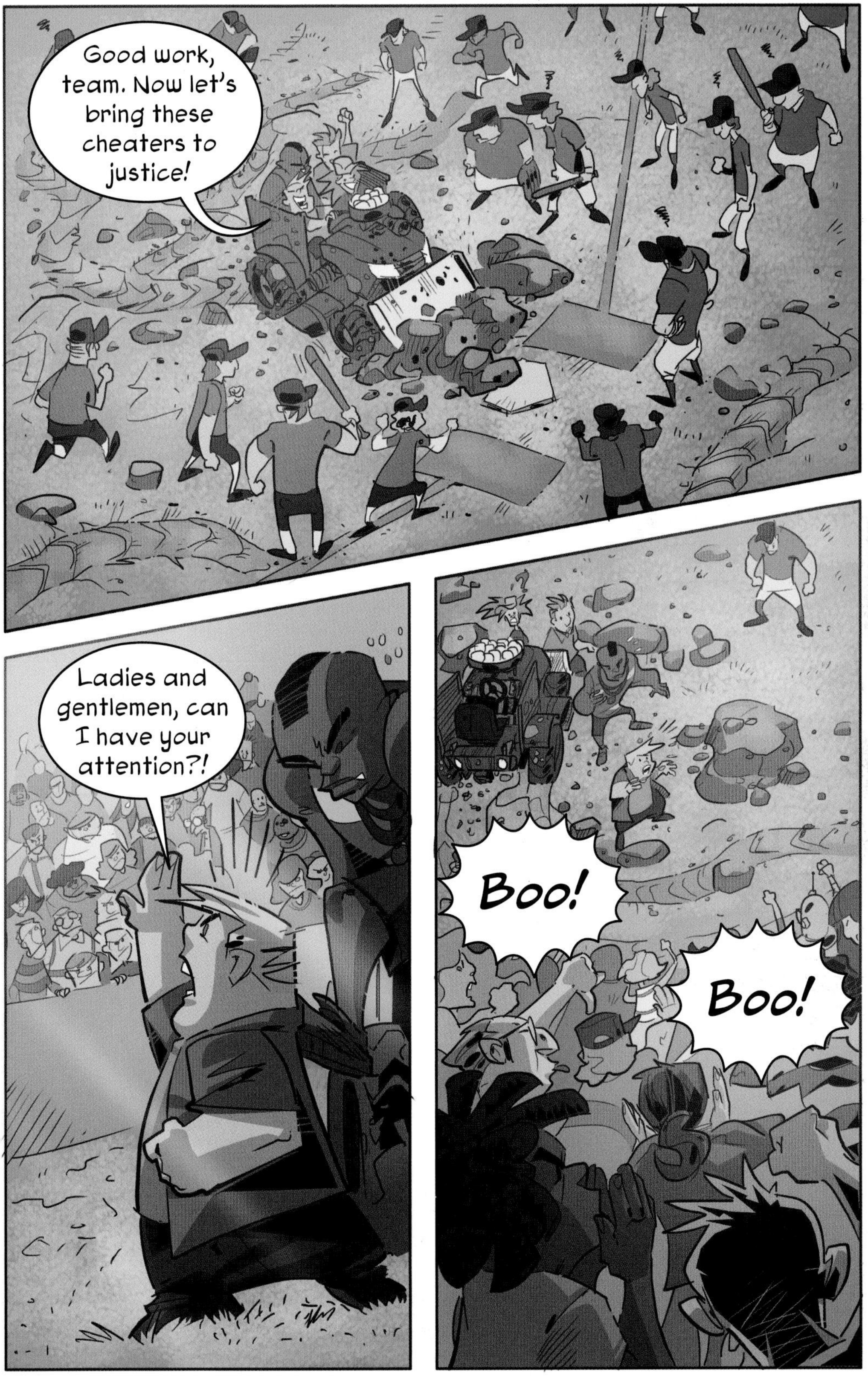
Good work, team. Now let's bring these cheaters to justice!
Ladies and gentlemen, can I have your attention?!
Boo!
Boo!

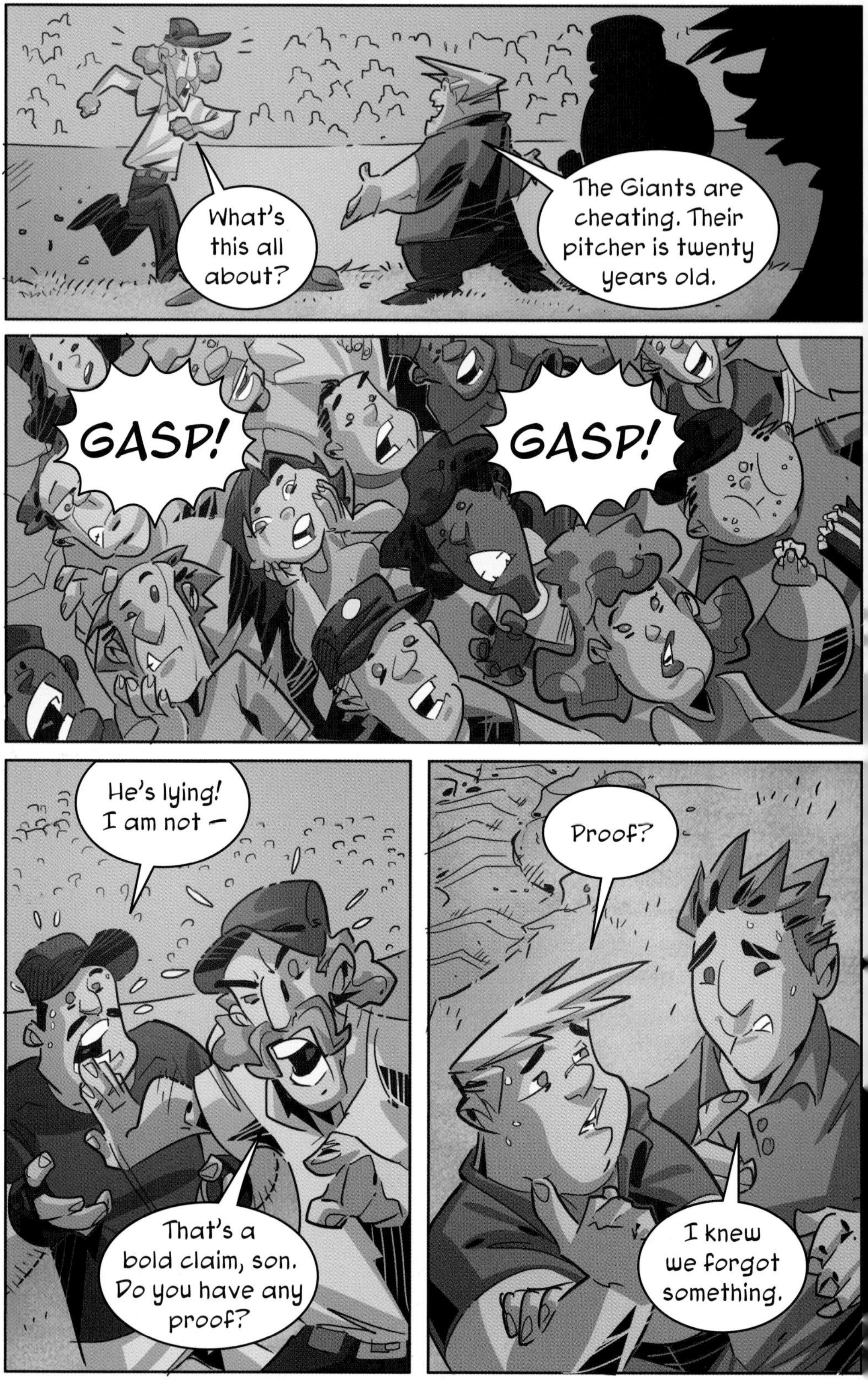
What's this all about?
The Giants are cheating. Their pitcher is twenty years old.
GASP!
GASP!
He's lying! I am not —
That's a bold claim, son. Do you have any proof?
Proof?
I knew we forgot something.

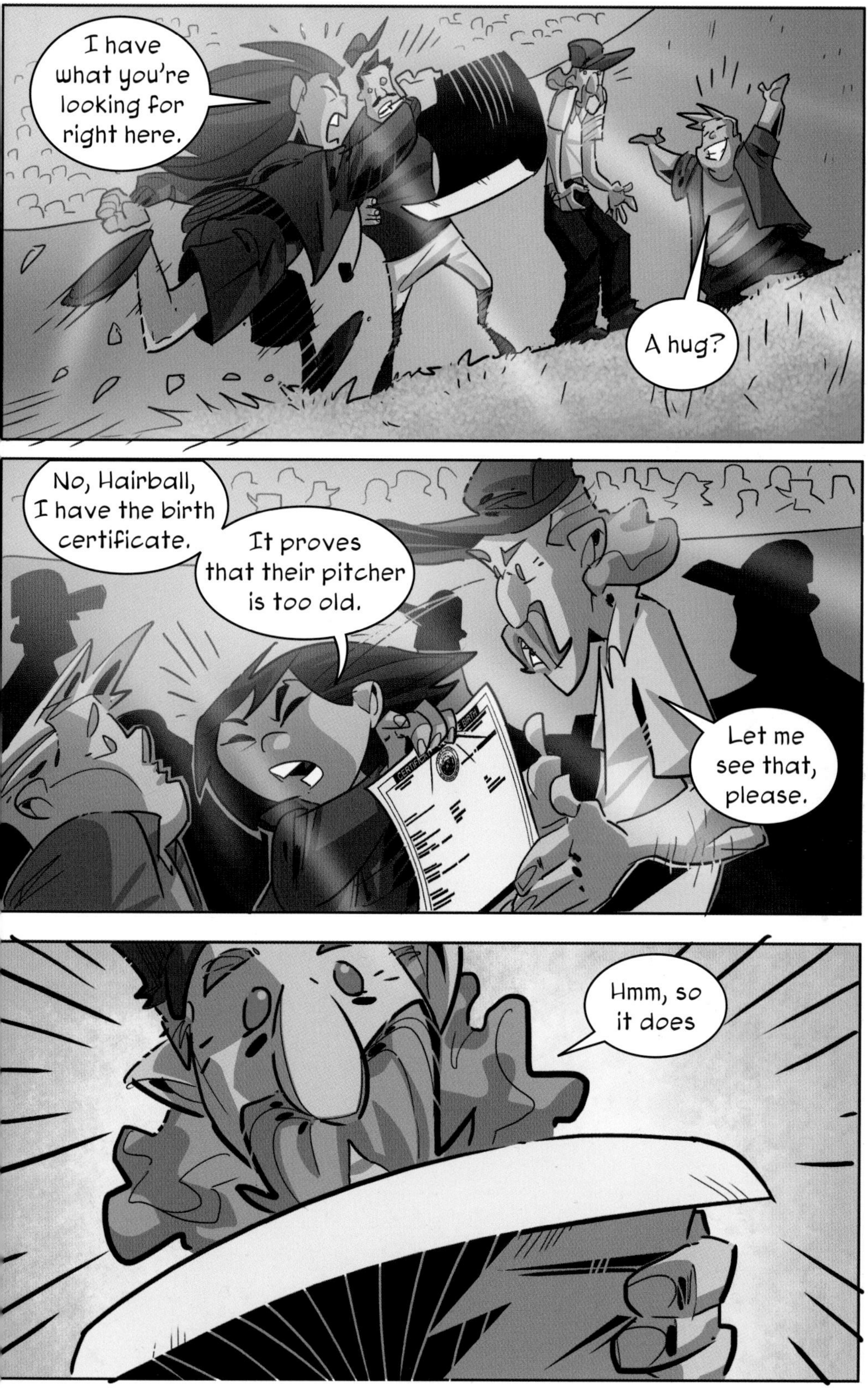
I have what you're looking for right here.
A hug?
No, Hairball, I have the birth certificate.
It proves that their pitcher is too old.
Let me see that, please.
Hmm, so it does

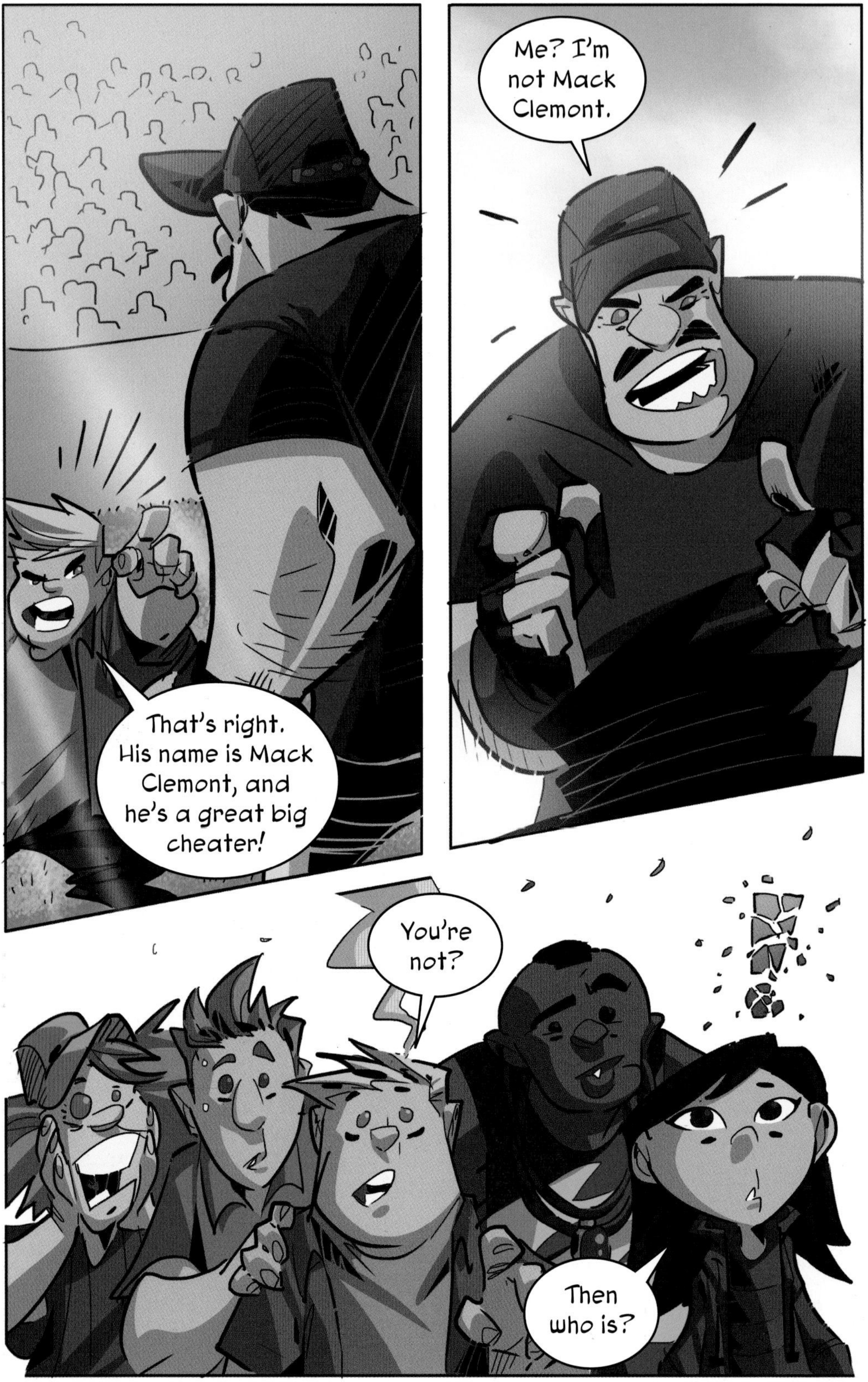
That's right. His name is Mack Clemont, and he's a great big cheater!
Me? I'm not Mack Clemont.
You're not?
Then who is?

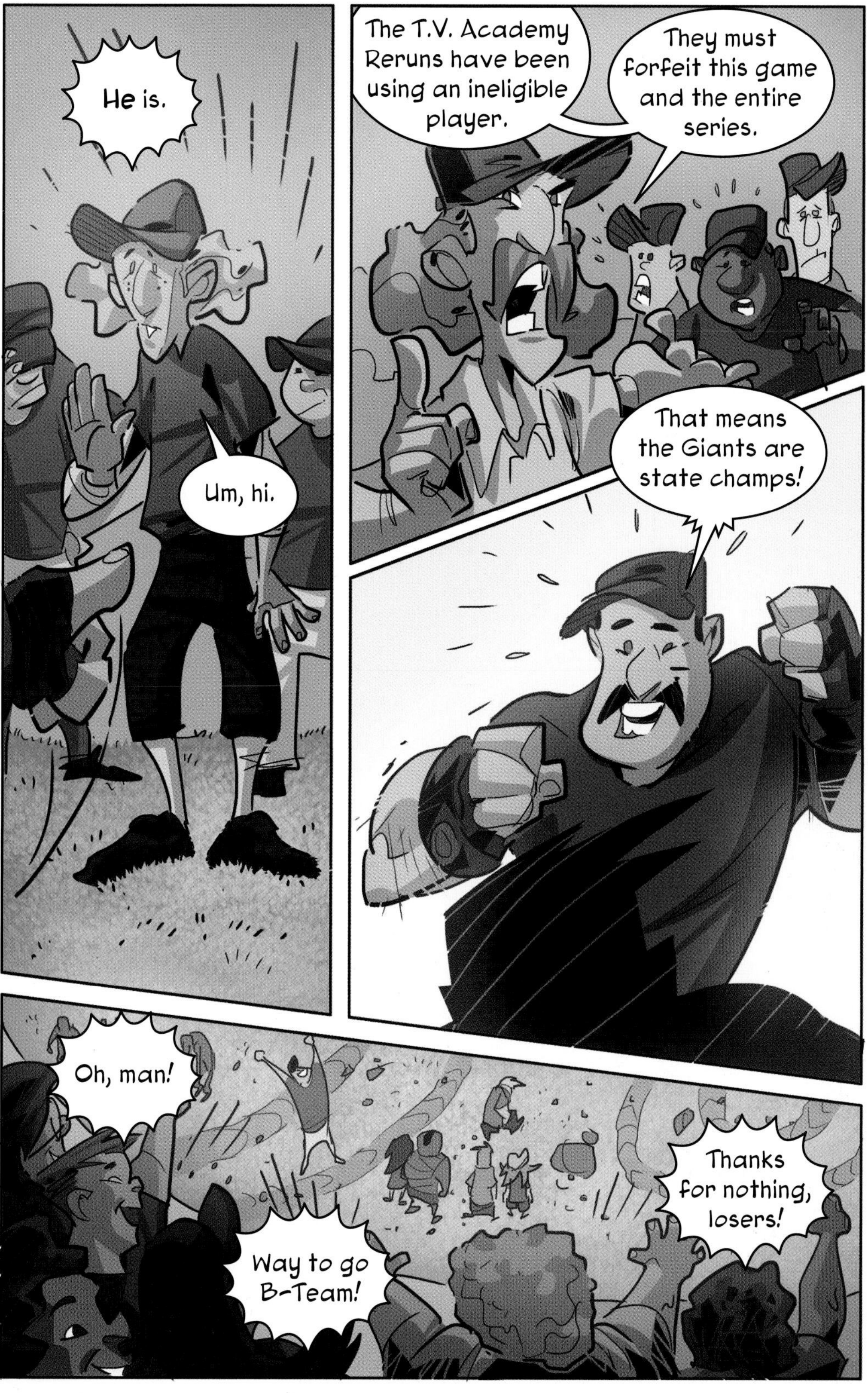
He is.
Um, hi.
The T.V. Academy Reruns have been using an ineligible player.
They must forfeit this game and the entire series.
That means the Giants are state champs!
Oh, man!
Thanks for nothing, losers!
Way to go B-Team!

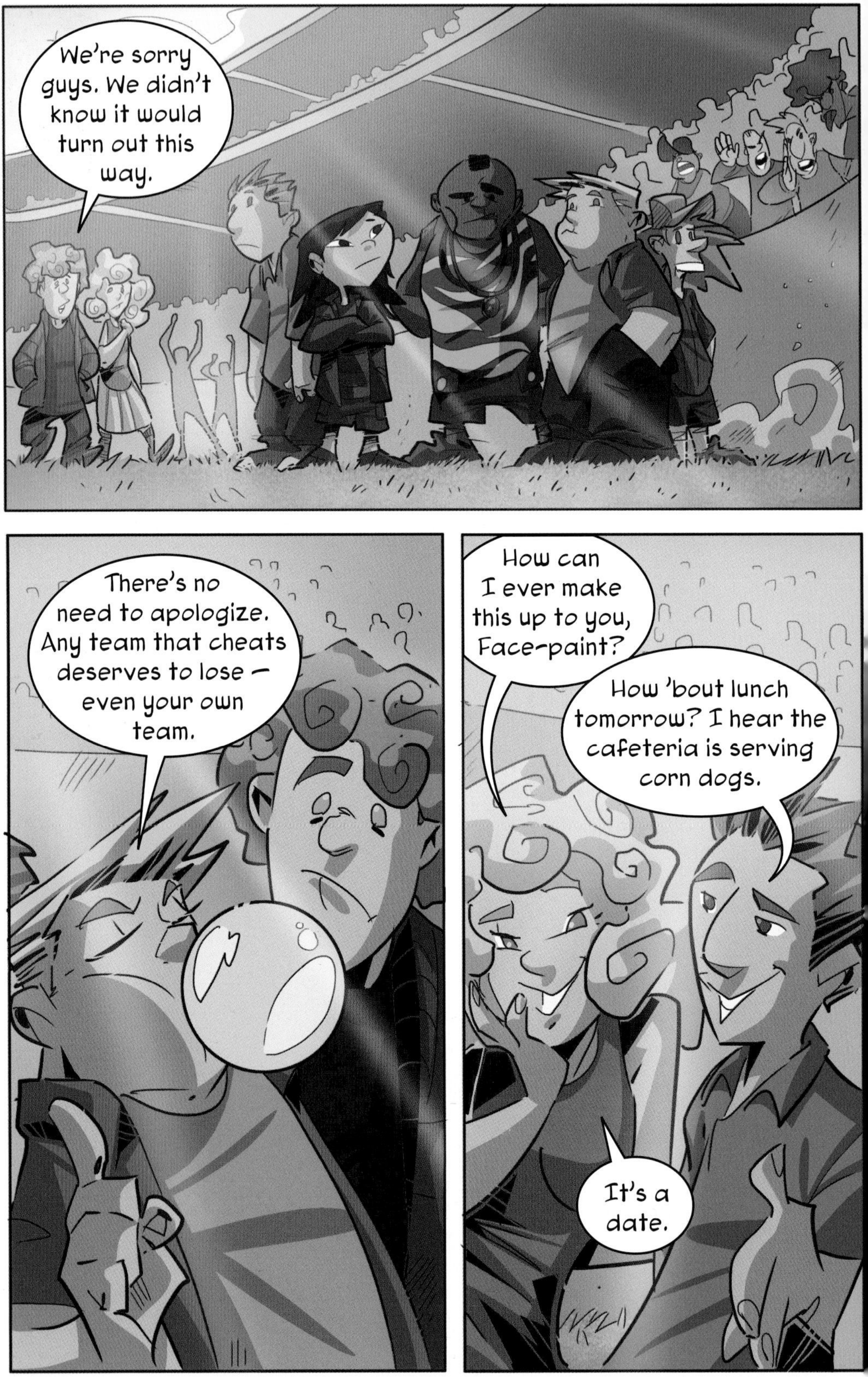
We're sorry guys. We didn't know it would turn out this way.
There's no need to apologize. Any team that cheats deserves to lose — even your own team.
How can I ever make this up to you, Face-paint?
How 'bout lunch tomorrow? I hear the cafeteria is serving corn dogs.
It's a date.

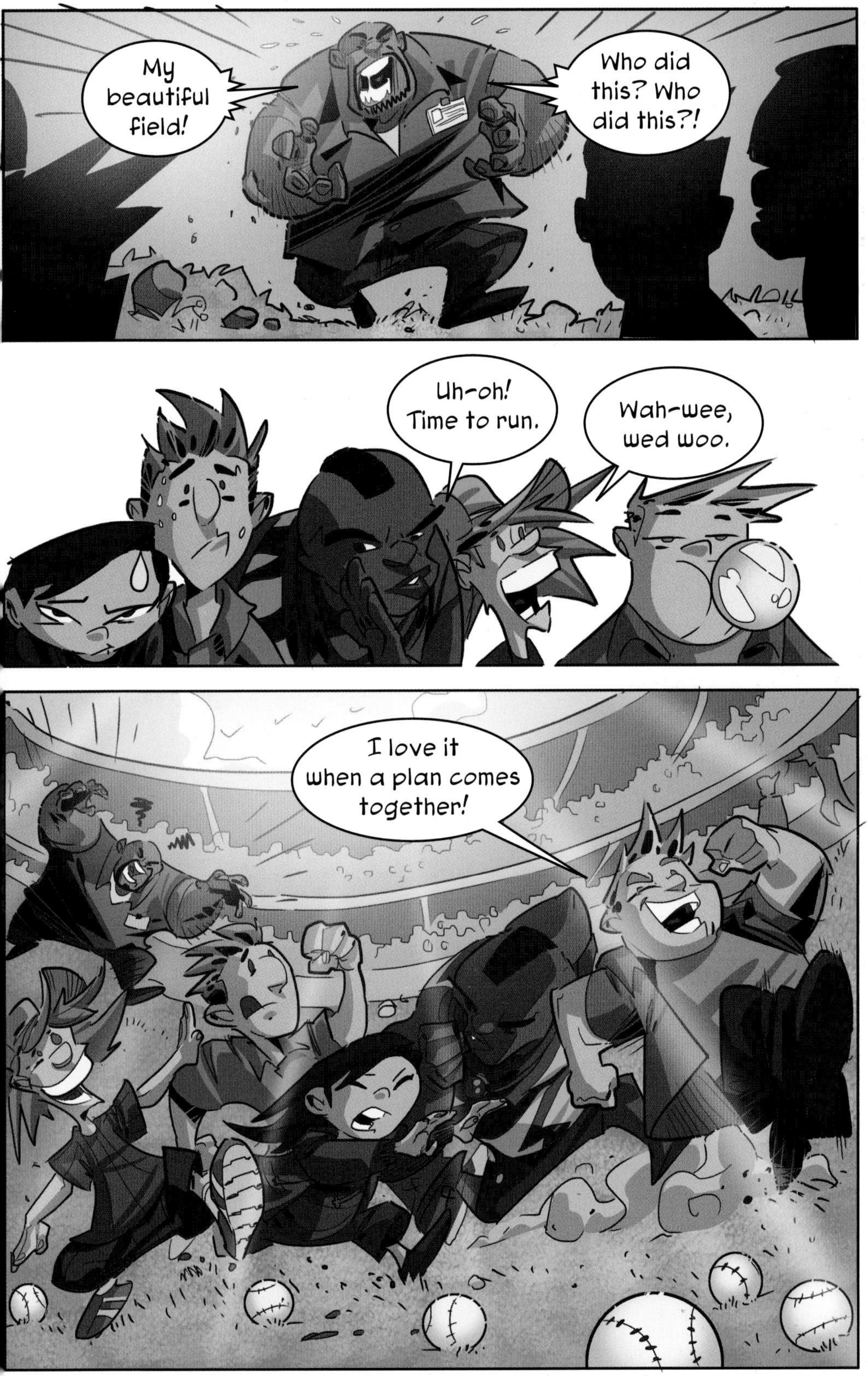
My beautiful field!
Who did this? Who did this?!
Uh-oh! Time to run.
Wah-wee, wed woo.
I love it when a plan comes together!

AT BAT WITH . . .

THE B-TEAM

FOUR STUDENT ATHLETES WERE CUT FROM THEIR TEAMS, BUT THEY DIDN'T GIVE UP. THEY CREATED THE ULTIMATE FAN CLUB . . . THE B-TEAM, WHO WILL STOP AT NOTHING TO HELP THEIR FORMER SQUADS WIN.

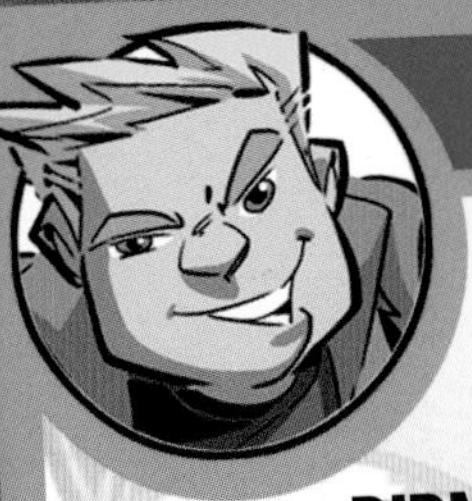

HAIRBALL

BIRTHPLACE: RENO, NEVADA
FORMER SPORT: FOOTBALL

DIDN'T MAKE THE CUT BECAUSE . . .

ALTHOUGH A TALENTED PLAYER, HAIRBALL REFUSED TO RUIN HIS HAIRDO. EVENTUALLY, HIS PERFECT LOCKS MADE HAIRBALL UNABLE TO PUT ON A HELMET. HIS REFUSAL TO MESS HIS HAIR GOT HIM CUT FROM HIS FAVORITE SPORT.

FACE-PAINT

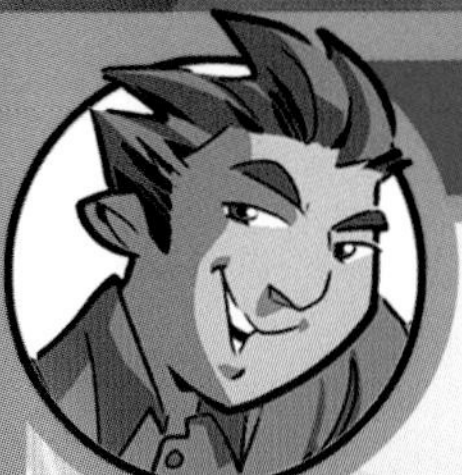

BIRTHPLACE: RENO, NEVADA
FORMER SPORT: BASKETBALL

DIDN'T MAKE THE CUT BECAUSE . . .

FACE-PAINT REFUSED TO GO UP FOR A REBOUND. WHEN HIS COACHED ASKED HIM WHY, FACE-PAINT REPLIED, "I CAN'T RISK INJURING THIS MASTERPIECE!" HE WAS TALKING ABOUT HIS PRETTY FACE.

HOWLING MOUTH

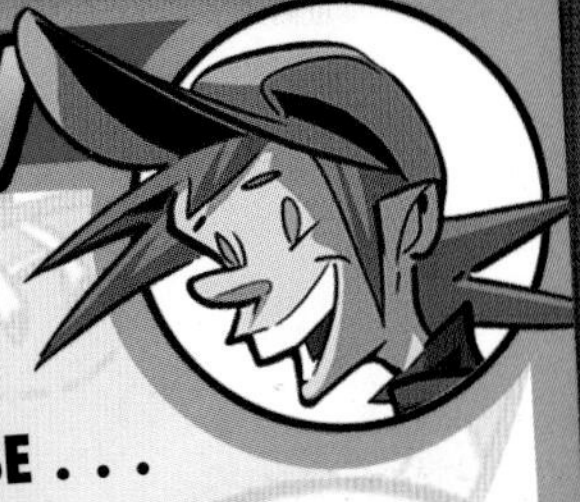

BIRTHPLACE: RENO, NEVADA
FORMER SPORT: BASEBALL

DIDN'T MAKE THE CUT BECAUSE . . .

ACTUALLY HE DID! AFTER TRYOUTS, HOWLING MOUTH NOTICED HIS NAME WASN'T ON THE TEAM ROSTER. HE GOT SO MAD, HE CHEWED OUT THE COACH. THE COACH MEANT TO INCLUDE HOWLING MOUTH ON THE LIST – BUT, AFTER BEING YELLED AT, DECIDED TO CUT HIM INSTEAD.

R.U. WITTUS

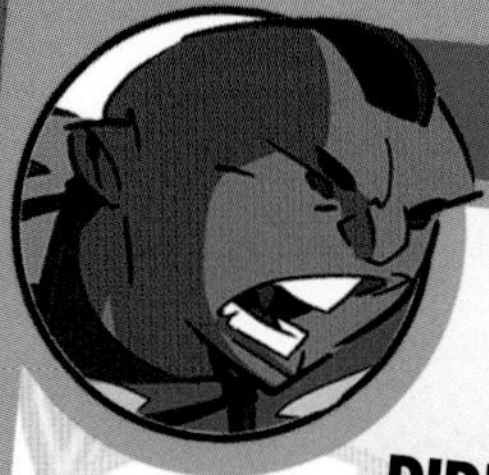

BIRTHPLACE: RENO, NEVADA
FORMER SPORT: WRESTLING

DIDN'T MAKE THE CUT BECAUSE . . .

HE WAS TOO STRONG! R.U. COULD TAKE DOWN THE ENTIRE WRESTLING TEAM WITH ONE ARM TIED BEHIND HIS BACK. HE QUICKLY GREW TIRED OF PINNING HIS OPPONENTS WITH HIS PINKY FINGER. SINCE HE WAS NO LONGER GIVING 110%, THE COACH KICKED HIM OFF THE TEAM.

AUTHOR

RYAN JACOBSON IS THE AUTHOR OF MORE THAN A DOZEN CHILDREN'S BOOKS. HE WORKS AS A BOOK EDITOR AND MARKETING SPECIALIST FOR A SMALL PRESS, AND HE HAS EXTENSIVE EXPERIENCE WORKING WITH CHILDREN, DATING BACK TO HIS DAYS AS A SUMMER CAMP COUNSELOR. RYAN LIVES WITH HIS WIFE LORA AND THEIR SONS, JONAH AND LUCAS.

ILLUSTRATOR

IN 1989, EDUARDO FERRARA STARTED IN THE FIELD OF ILLUSTRATION AS AN ASSISTANT PROFESSOR AT THE SCHOOL OF DESIGN GRAPHICS IN SAO PAULO, BRAZIL. SINCE THEN, HE'S BEEN A FREELANCE ILLUSTRATOR FOR VARIOUS ADVERTISING AGENCIES, PUBLISHERS, AND STUDIOS, PRODUCING ILLUSTRATIONS, PACKAGING, STORYBOARDS, CARDS, CHARACTERS, AND COMICS.

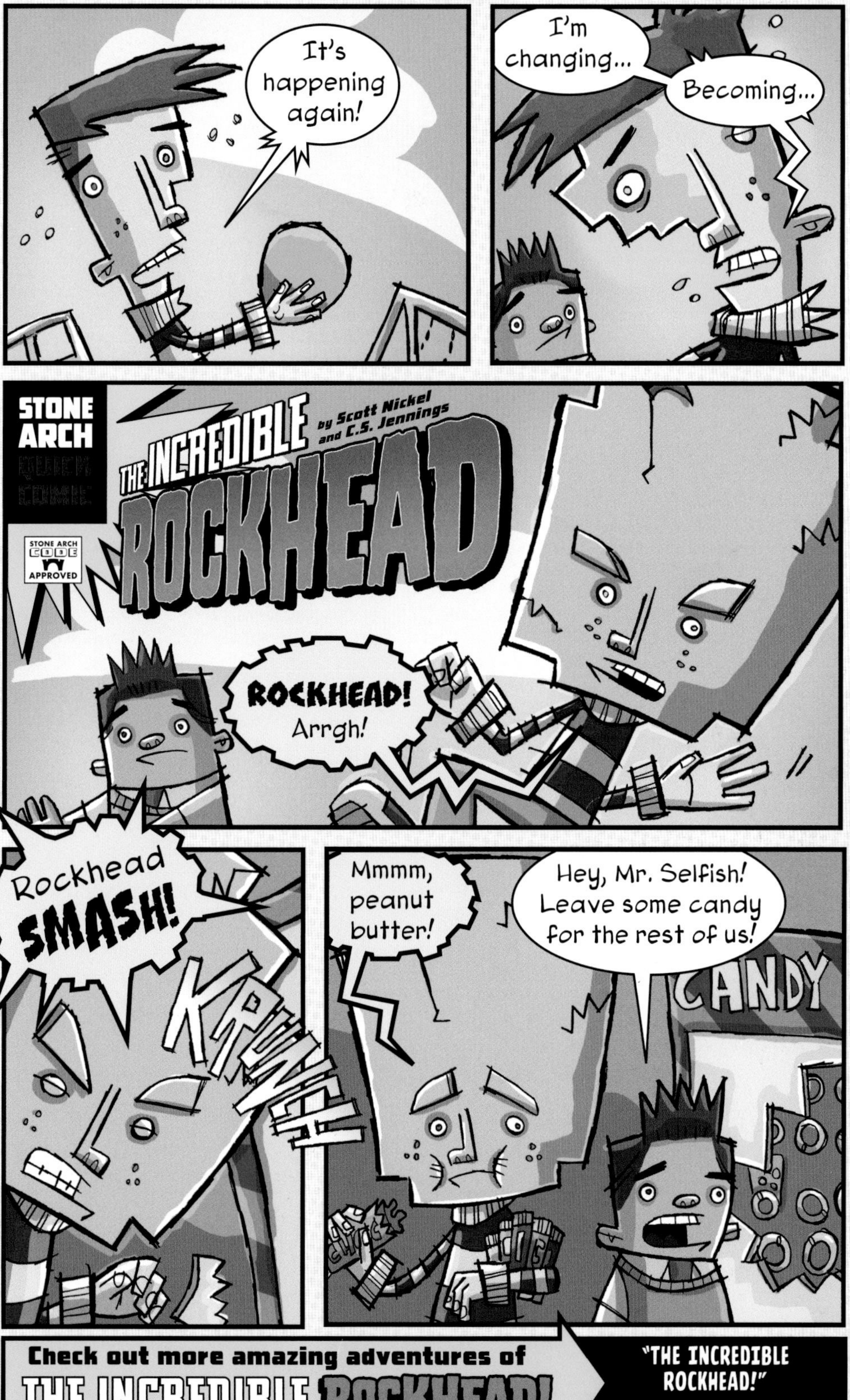
It's happening again!
I'm changing...
Becoming...
STONE ARCH
THE INCREDIBLE ROCKHEAD
by Scott Nickel and C.S. Jennings
STONE ARCH CODE APPROVED
ROCKHEAD! Arrgh!
Rockhead SMASH!
KRUNCH
Mmmm, peanut butter!
Hey, Mr. Selfish! Leave some candy for the rest of us!
CANDY
Check out more amazing adventures of
THE INCREDIBLE ROCKHEAD!
"THE INCREDIBLE ROCKHEAD!"
"THE DOZER STRIKES!"

DISCUSSION QUESTIONS

1. WHICH MEMBER OF THE B-TEAM IS YOUR FAVORITE? WHY?

2. IF YOU FIND OUT THAT YOUR TEAMMATES ARE CHEATING, SHOULD YOU TELL ON THEM? WHY OR WHY NOT?

3. THE B-TEAM CAUSED THEIR OWN TEAM TO LOSE. DO YOU THINK THEY SHOULD BE REWARDED OR PUNISHED? EXPLAIN.

WRITING PROMPTS

1. IMAGINE YOU ARE FORMING YOUR OWN B-TEAM. WHICH OF YOUR FRIENDS WOULD YOU RECRUIT TO JOIN YOUR SQUAD? WHAT KINDS OF SKILLS DO YOUR TEAM MEMBERS HAVE THAT WOULD HELP SOLVE MYSTERIES? WRITE ABOUT IT.

2. HAIRBALL LEADS THE B-TEAM. ARE YOU A LEADER? WHAT KINDS OF THINGS HAVE YOU DONE THAT MIGHT MAKE YOU A GOOD ROLE MODEL FOR OTHERS? WRITE ABOUT SOME TIMES WHEN YOU SET A GOOD EXAMPLE FOR OTHER PEOPLE.

GLOSSARY

BOLD (BOHLD)—SHOWING NO FEAR OF DANGER

CROWNED (KROUND)—DECLARED SOMEONE TO BE THE WINNER

DISGUISES (diss-GIZE-iz)—IF YOU PUT ON A DISGUISE, YOU DRESS IN A WAY THAT HIDES YOUR IDENTITY

EQUIPMENT (i-KWIP-muhnt)—THE TOOLS AND MACHINES NEEDED FOR A PARTICULAR PURPOSE

FORFEIT (FOR-fit)—GIVE UP OR LOSE

INELIGIBLE (in-EL-uh-juh-buhl)—IF YOU ARE INELIGIBLE, YOU DO NOT MEET THE REQUIREMENTS

JUSTICE (JUHSS-tiss)—FAIR AND IMPARTIAL JUDGMENT

PICKLE (PIK-uhl)—A DIFFICULT SITUATION, OR A SITUATION IN BASEBALL WHERE A BASERUNNER IS CAUGHT IN A RUNDOWN

PITY (PIT-ee)—FEELING SORRY OR SYMPATHY

RECOGNIZE (REK-uhg-nize)—TO SEE SOMEONE AND KNOW WHO THE PERSON IS

RUIN (ROO-in)—TO SPOIL OR DESTROY SOMEONE

SURROUNDED (suh-ROUN-did)—ENCLOSED ON ALL SIDES

THRIVE (THRIVE)—TO DO WELL AND FLOURISH

THE FUN DOESN'T STOP HERE!

Discover more:

- VIDEOS & CONTESTS!
- GAMES & PUZZLES!
- HEROES & VILLAINS!
- AUTHORS & ILLUSTRATORS!

@ www.capstonekids.com

FIND COOL WEBSITES AND MORE BOOKS LIKE THIS ONE
AT WWW.FACTHOUND.COM JUST TYPE IN BOOK I.D.
9781434226068 AND YOU'RE READY TO GO!

◤◥ STONE ARCH BOOKS™

Published in 2011
A Capstone Imprint
151 Good Counsel Drive, P.O. Box 669
Mankato, Minnesota 56002
www.capstonepub.com

Cataloging-in-Publication Data is available at the
Library of Congress website.

ISBN: 978-1-4342-2606-8 (library binding)
ISBN: 978-1-4342-3068-3 (paperback)

Summary: Four student athletes are cut from
their teams, but they're determined not to
give up.

Designer: Brann Garvey
Art Director: Bob Lentz
Editor: Donald Lemke
Production Specialist: Michelle Biedscheid
Creative Director: Heather Kindseth
Editorial Director: Michael Dahl
Publisher: Lori Benton

Printed in the United States of America
in Stevens Point, Wisconsin.
092010   005934WZS11